BAD SCENE

BAD SCENE

Basil Copper

Chivers Press • G.K. Hall & Co.
Bath, England   Thorndike, Maine USA

This Large Print edition is published by Chivers Press, England, and by G.K. Hall & Co., USA.

Published in 2000 in the U.K. by arrangement with the author.

Published in 2000 in the U.S. by arrangement with Basil Copper.

U.K. Hardcover   ISBN 0-7540-4117-4   (Chivers Large Print)
U.K. Softcover   ISBN 0-7540-4118-2   (Camden Large Print)
U.S. Softcover   ISBN 0-7838-8997-6   (Nightingale Series Edition)

The text of this Large Print edition is unabridged.
Other aspects of the book may vary from the original edition.

Set in 16 pt. New Times Roman.

Printed in Great Britain on acid-free paper.

British Library Cataloguing in Publication Data available

Library of Congress Cataloging-in-Publication Data

Copper, Basil.
    Bad scene / Basil Copper.
       p.   (large print)   cm.
    ISBN 0-7838-8997-6 (lg. print : sc : alk. paper)
    1. Faraday, Mike (Fictitious character)—Fiction. 2. Private investigators—California—Los Angeles—Fiction. 3. Los Angeles (Calif.)—Fiction. 4. Large type books. I. Title.
PR6053.O658 B34   2000
823'.914—dc21   00–021438

CHAPTER ONE

1

Alex Prosser was a gigantic, 20-stone, red-faced man dressed in a faded blue and white stripe yachting sweater, his blue matching cap with its tarnished gold badge pushed back on top of his carroty hair as he leaned forward, threatening the breaking strain of the client's chair the other side my desk.

The sweat shone in among the roots of his hair and glazed the freckles on his face as he furrowed his features up and down in what was meant to be an intellectual expression. Stella had gone out for the afternoon and I was alone in the office when he showed. I vaguely knew of him from contacts in Ocean Beach and other places up and down the coast.

He was a charter skipper and boat-builder in business for himself, running and maintaining power craft, along with two of his brothers who were built a little less like King Kong. But I didn't sell him short. Prosser was a shrewd businessman and he had it up there between his ears all right, despite his ape-like appearance.

Now his faded blue eyes that matched the sweater and his cap were troubled. He licked his lips like he could still taste the salt spray on them. In fact he was so nautical that I looked around for his brass-bound telescope and the parrot but he seemed to have left them home today.

'There was this girl, Mr Faraday,' he said for the third time.

I sighed.

'There's always a girl, Mr Prosser.'

He nodded portentously.

'That's true, Mr Faraday. Call me Alex.'

I nodded.

'My name's Mike. Now let's get down to cases.'

It had been a rough quarter and any assignment other than stake-out would have been welcome this time of year. Any time of year, come to that. I only hoped he didn't want to consult me about a grunion run. I knew next to nothing about fishing or nautical matters. I left that to Stella, who sails a fast off-shore ketch when she's not tending my business.

Prosser shifted his vast bulk in the chair again, causing it to creak like it was about to go through the floor into the office below. I was full of no coffee, my butt sore from polishing the seat of my chair, but I had a feeling there was something serious in back of Prosser's visit. He wouldn't have come up from the coast this afternoon to see me for purely social reasons.

I shifted my own position and frowned at the cracks in the ceiling through the thin blue haze of my cigarette smoke. The plastic-bladed fan went on pecking at the brittle edges of the silence, redistributing the tired air, while the stalled traffic on the boulevard below the window added to the charm of L.A. that somehow always gets left out the tourist brochures.

'There was a girl,' I prompted him.

'Sure,' he said gloomily.

'She's the least of my problems.'

'That's what I'm here for,' I said. 'To listen to problems. Fire away.'

Prosser hesitated and then went hurrying on like he'd lose the thread if he didn't do it in one go.

'I was hired a few weeks ago,' he went on. 'To take this guy out to a private island up the coast. It's a small one, called Cocos. You know it?'

I shrugged.

'There's thousands of islands along the coast of California, Mr Prosser. A good many of them are private.'

The big man shifted again in the chair, making an ear-splitting cracking noise.

'I get all sorts of queer customers in my business. My boat-hire manager put this guy on to me. I guess he maybe felt uneasy about taking him out himself.'

'Why was that?' I said.

Prosser raised his big shoulders.

'He was a well-dressed guy, with a hard face.

But there was something about him. He never smiled. I figured he might not be on the up and up.'

I grinned.

'What makes you say so?'

A defensive look passed across Prosser's face.

'Just a hunch, Mr Faraday. That's another sense you develop in my business. Like yours, I guess.'

'Maybe,' I said. 'You're trying to tell me in a polite way that this character was maybe a racketeer. Why didn't you refuse the hire?'

It was Prosser's turn to smile.

'Look here, Mr Faraday, times are hard. The boat business is no exception. We got a lot of opposition with big combines. Maybe this guy was a racketeer. It wasn't my job to ask him questions. It was just a feeling.'

'All right,' I said. 'He got a name?'

'He told me Mr Brown,' Prosser said shortly. 'He signed the book, giving his initial and an address in Chicago.'

'We won't worry about that,' I said. 'What happened next?'

'We fixed a price for me to take him out to Cocos,' Prosser went on. 'It's a ways up the coast from my place and I wondered why he hadn't fixed on an outfit situated a little nearer. But like I said I don't argue with the customers.'

'This character had transport?' I said.

4

The big man nodded.

'I guess so, Mr Faraday. Though I didn't see it. Anyway we went out there after dark. He specified that. The trip took about five hours. Mr Brown hardly spoke, though I gave him food and whisky like I always do with my private hire clients.'

'You had any other crew on board?' I said.

Again Prosser shook his head.

'I usually work two-handed but Brown said he only wanted me along. So I upped the rate.'

'Naturally,' I said. 'This Brown have any luggage?'

'Nothing to speak of. Just a topcoat against the wind which he carried over his arm until we got out in the bay; and a small black briefcase like businessmen carry. We got there all right and I left him at a small landing stage. There was a big guy with an Alsatian dog to meet him. The big guy told me to stand off and anchor somewhere and come back in two hours. It was past midnight then and I was a little sore.'

'But you anchored somewhere and hit your bunk for a couple hours,' I said.

'That's about it, Mr Faraday. When I got back to the jetty only the big guy showed. He said Mr Brown was staying overnight and that they'd run him back. He paid me my fee and gave me a hundred bucks on top so I didn't argue.'

I gave Prosser one of my long, steady looks. 'Who owns Cocos?'

'No idea, Mr Faraday. Some millionaire, I guess.'

Prosser leaned forward across the desk.

'Nothing else happened for a week and I'd almost forgotten about Cocos and my passenger when this girl turned up one afternoon. Good-looking kid with long, blonde hair. About twenty-two, I should have said. She was looking for Mr Brown and asked if I'd seen him. I told her like I told you.'

I set fire to a cigarette and blew out blue smoke toward the ceiling.

'She got a name too?'

Prosser didn't exactly smirk but he made an expression that got near to it.

'Miss Green. Pretty funny, eh?'

'Hilarious,' I said. 'I suppose her Christian name wasn't Violet?'

Prosser gurgled to himself before becoming serious again.

'I didn't ask her, Mr Faraday. She went off eventually and the matter dropped from my mind. But I been thinking the last couple of days. That's why I came to you.'

'There's more, then?' I said.

There were strange shadows in back of Prosser's eyes now.

'Sure, Mr Faraday. Plenty more. Two nights ago someone tried to murder me.'

I put my spent match-stalk in the earthenware tray on my desk.

'That's interesting,' I said.

'Too interesting for my blood,' Prosser said.

He put two hands as big as baseball bats down on the desk in front of him and studied his massive nails. They were bitten almost to the quick though I didn't figure him for a nervous type.

'This would have to be an assault with a weapon,' I said. 'A man like you wouldn't be afraid of physical violence.'

'That's right,' Prosser said. 'It's out of my league. More in your line. Besides, apart from the inconvenience, it would be too difficult for me to run my business from the bottom of the bay.'

'There is that,' I admitted.

'Call me Alex,' he said again.

I decided to humour him.

'What do your brothers think about this, Alex?'

The big man shrugged.

'I don't involve them in the gritty end. One's trained as an accountant. He handles the tax and business side. The other has a degree in engineering, designs the boats and services the equipment. They're both better educated than me.'

'Don't sell yourself short, Alex,' I said.

'You're the senior partner, aren't you? And they're working for you.'

Alex Prosser grinned.

'You have a point, Mr Faraday. Where was I?'

'Being murdered,' I said. 'Tell me about it. And the name's Mike.'

There was a faint pallor beneath the reddened surface of Prosser's facial skin now. He pursed up his lips like the memory of it was too painful for recollection.

'You know that section up around Palos Verdes, Mike?'

'It's a big area,' I said. 'Refresh my memory.'

'We got quite an operation up there. Prosser Marine. Everyone on that part of the coast knows us. I'll give you one of my business cards.'

'I'm still not quite sure what you want me to do,' I said.

Prosser shrugged.

'Apart from preventing me getting my arse shot off, you mean?'

'There is that,' I said.

Prosser gave me a wry smile.

'I'm coming to it. You'll just have to let me tell it my own way.'

'Who's trying to stop you?' I said.

'Well, I'd almost forgotten about this girl, like I said,' Prosser went on.

'But you'd recognise her again?' I said.

8

The big man nodded.

'Sure. Pretty girls on the coast are two a penny but she was something special.'

He was breathing heavily through his nose now and there was a sudden white look about the mouth and eyes like the memory of two nights before was bugging him.

'We got a pier up there, Mike,' he went on after a minute or so. 'What I mean is it's a private pier, belonging to us. We got offices and workshops there and a proper boatyard adjoining. We keep a lot of our working boats and hire craft out on the pier, to leeward of course, in case it blows, but it's fairly shallow there and there isn't much of a tidal drop.'

He broke off.

'I don't know why I'm telling you all this.'

'Because you like to be thorough, Alex,' I said.

He dredged up a faint smile.

'Maybe,' he said softly. 'Well, I went out along the pier like I often do, around ten p.m. Me and my brothers all got houses in back of the beach, in sight of the yard. That way it's pretty convenient.'

'Sure,' I said.

'I was taking a general look round, checking the moorings, that sort of thing. I surprised someone on the *Glory B*. That's the deep-sea launch I regard as my own. He was trying to force the companionway door.

'I shouted at him and he turned around. He

fired at me point-blank with a big cannon. If I hadn't stumbled getting down on to the deck he'd have taken the top of my head off.'

CHAPTER TWO

1

'Nasty,' I said.

Prosser nodded.

'You can say that again.'

There was an ugly silence in the office now and I waited for him to go on, not interrupting. He swallowed once or twice, running a big-fingered hand over the rivulets of sweat that were suddenly streaming down his face.

'I landed on the deck face down, Mike. I guess I was half-stunned, both with the force of the explosion and the impact with the deck. When I came around the big guy was gone. I examined the door of the companionway but apart from scratches in the teak surround there was no damage done.'

'What was this character like?' I said.

Prosser shrugged.

'Big guy with a hard face. I only caught a glimpse by the pistol-flash. It was my impression he had greasy black hair. He wore some sort of leather jacket despite the heat of the night.'

'Could fit hundreds of people,' I said. 'What would he want aboard your boat? And how would this tie in with the girl and your trip to Cocos?'

The giant gave me a slightly regretful look.

'I'm coming to it, like I said. My thoughts were pretty tangled at the time but they started getting clearer the more I mulled things over in my mind.'

'You told your wife about this?' I said. 'You have a wife, I take it?'

Alex Prosser nodded.

'Sure,' he said easily. 'Who hasn't? But I didn't want to worry her. I just told my brothers I'd spotted someone prowling around the moored craft and warned them to keep their eyes open.'

'You played it right,' I said. 'But I still don't know why you didn't ring the police.'

The big man put his hambone hands down on the desk surface again and studied his nails dispassionately.

'There are a number of reasons, Mike. Like I said I didn't want to worry my wife. Maybe this was just some crazy junkie looking for a place to sleep and so hopped up he didn't care who he killed. The L.A. basin is crawling with people like that now.'

I nodded.

'Or?'

Prosser gave me a strange little twisted smile that seemed to linger at the corners of his mouth for some time.

'Well, it all ties in, Mike,' he said at last. 'I take Brown out to Cocos. He looks a hard case. He doesn't show when I'm supposed to pick him up. There's another guy there with a guard dog who tells me to go about my business.'

'I follow all that,' I said. 'And the girl. She was looking for Brown so she had a lead on you and your boat. But the guy with the gun could mean anything. Or nothing. Though I admit there was a lot of action centring around you after Brown showed up. You tried to trace him since?'

Prosser shook his head grimly.

'I had no need to, Mr Faraday. I'll explain that in a little while. But the big man turned up only three-four days after my talk with the girl. I can't be certain of the dates. But if a guy's trying to break into someone else's property he doesn't usually try to kill the owner. He'd talk his way out, surely; pretend he was half-drunk; or had made a genuine mistake. The more I thought it over the more it seemed like a trained killer to me.'

I nodded again.

'You were at the rough end, so it would sure as hell look like that to you. It looks like that to me at the moment. But why would he want to enter your boat? He didn't think the girl was there, surely. This is all supposition, of course.'

There were little glints in Prosser's eyes now.

'Of course, Mike, but your mind is working the same way mine is. Tie the three things together and we've maybe got something.'

I gave him one of my best crooked grins.

'You already got Brown and Green. Maybe your visitor was Mr Black.'

Prosser smiled but it was a little strained. So would mine have been in his position.

'Let's leave that for the moment,' I said. 'We can't get any farther on supposition. You said you had no need to trace Brown just now.'

The shadows were back in Prosser's eyes. He rummaged around in his hip pocket, shifting on the client's chair so that it gave out tortured squeaks with his weight.

'I got something here, Mr Faraday. I bought the late edition of the *Examiner* last night, from a kiosk along the beach road. It gave me a hell of a jolt I can tell you.'

I waited while he rummaged around in a much scuffed leather billfold he took from his pants pocket.

'How did you get on to me?' I said.

Prosser grunted, the gold badge on his blue yachting cap glinting beneath the light of the overhead lamp.

'I saw your ad on an inside page of the *Examiner* in that box with the heavy type around it. You seemed the right sort of guy for me.'

I grinned.

'So someone does read them.'

Prosser grunted again, throwing a crumpled cutting over toward me. It took up a quarter page, including the text and a couple of photo shots. I stared at it for a long moment. I'd seen a lot of bullet holes in my time but even allowing for the somewhat blurred picture this guy had them in spades.

There was an edge of excitement in Prosser's voice that hadn't been there before.

'That was my client, Mike! Mr Brown. The character I took out to Cocos Island. He was fished out the bay a couple of days back, just like you see him there. Looks like murder all right.'

'Moths didn't make those holes,' I said, squinting at the picture again.

'How about it, Mr Faraday,' Prosser said, forgetting we were on Christian name terms. 'I could be next. You want to take the case?'

I looked at him through half-closed eyelids.

'I just took it,' I said.

2

It was late afternoon and I was checking through the *Examiner* cutting for the third time when Stella walked in. I'd been giving Prosser's story a lot of brain-time and thoughts were whirling around my think-tank like a pinball machine on Saturday night. Maybe the man in the leather jacket wanted to take out a 20-stone giant without any further argument. Maybe. Or perhaps there was some other explanation.

15

Because he figured Prosser was tied in with Brown for some reason? Assuming all this connected up and Mr Black wasn't a simple prowler. I sat hunched over the desk, my cigarette smoke rising toward the cracks in the ceiling, aware that Stella was watching me as she hung her lightweight raincoat on the stand in the corner. I stood it for a second longer and then decided to crack.

'Don't tell me you had a customer,' she said.

I grinned.

'A big one,' I said. 'Pity you missed out.'

Stella raised an elegant eyebrow. It didn't affect her beauty any.

'Don't tell me IBM has noticed our ad at last.'

I decided to ignore that. It was too hot this afternoon and I was still full of no coffee. Today Stella was wearing what she called one of her working outfits. She still looked terrific.

'I mean physically,' I said. 'He makes Carnera look like some effeminate ballet dancer.'

Stella's smile seemed to light up the whole office. She crossed over to the client's chair and sat down. She had on a fawn trouser suit that hugged her figure and in the open vee of her rust-coloured shirt she had a pale blue silk scarf. It sounds simple enough but it had my pulse throbbing all the way down to my socks. If you know what I mean.

The gold bell of her hair shimmered

16

beneath the overhead lamp as she put her head on one side and stared at me with very blue eyes.

'He got a name, Mike?' she said.

I nodded.

'I'll tell you all about it over coffee. You'll want to make notes.'

'I will?'

Stella's expression was bland and non-committal but she wasn't fooling me any. She got up and came around the desk to stand by my shoulder, looking down. That was pretty unnerving too. Just when I was beginning to crumble she leaned over and picked up Prosser's cutting from my blotter.

'This part of it?' she said.

'About two thirds,' I said. 'Like it says there the corpse's name was apparently Carl Brown, a businessman from Philadelphia. I have my doubts if what our client tells me is correct. He owns a boat firm and ran Brown out to Cocos Island about ten days before the guy was found floating in the bay in a perforated condition. Like you see there.'

'Like I see here,' Stella said, studying the cutting closely.

'There's a nasty echo this afternoon,' I said.

Stella smiled faintly but she went on reading just the same. I'd given up all hope when she went over to the glassed-in alcove where we brew up the coffee, with the brisk rat-tatting of high heels that always sends my blood-count

17

up. I sat back at my old broadtop and enjoyed the stale air the fan was circulating. It's a great way of making a living, Mike, I told myself.

Stella put her head round the screen, still with the cutting in her hand.

'I take it our client doesn't want the police involved, Mike? I can't find any reference to him here.'

'You take it right,' I said. 'Other things have happened since then. I can't say I blame him.'

There was a short silence and then I heard the click of the percolator going on. I sat back, salivating like one of Pavlov's dogs. I say this on every case but it's the only analogy that readily comes to mind.

'His name's Alex Prosser,' I said. 'He's a gigantic character who doesn't frighten easily. But he was plenty scared when he came to see me earlier today.'

'Pity I wasn't here,' Stella said.

'Which reminds me . . .' I started to say.

Stella interrupted me, briskly clattering cups and saucers.

'When I finished up checking that information at the Central Library, I found there was a sale on.'

I swivelled in my chair and looked at Stella critically. She was immaculate, like usual.

'You look great,' I said. 'What do you want with more clothes?'

Stella sighed like she was dealing with a mentality around three years old. She probably

18

was, in her book.

'It wasn't that sort of sale, goof. It was a marine store. There were some marvellous bargains. I got a lot of stuff for my sailboat. It's one of my hobbies at week-ends, remember?'

I swivelled back to face frontward again.

'I remember,' I said. 'And you stashed the stuff in the boot of your car.'

'I wasn't dragging it all the way up here,' Stella said.

She went back and finished making the coffee, putting the filled cup down on my blotter, going back for her own cup and the biscuit tin. Then she settled herself opposite and studied the cutting again. She had her scratchpad with her and from time to time she scribbled notes with her gold pen, her concentration making little frowning indentations between her immaculate eyebrows.

'So what's all this with Alex Prosser?' she said.

'Afterward,' I said. 'It's the coffee hour.'

Her smile still lingered as I started nuzzling into my cup.

CHAPTER THREE

1

I'd made an early start and the traffic was fairly light still when I tooled the Buick off the main stem and down on to the beach road at the intersection I wanted. It had been a two-hour drive up here and it was still only ten a.m., the sun hot and heavy on the windshield, the green-blue of the Pacific looking like a steel engraving as the sun caught the points of the wavelets farther out.

You're getting in one of your Emily Dickinson moods again, Mike, I told myself, as I waited at the junction on to the dusty beach road where the ice-cream shacks and coke-stands were already busy. At the water's edge, where the sand curved away in lemon yellow slices round the edge of the bay, the surf was black with the bobbing heads of swimmers while the mutton-chop foresails of small yachts were scattered across the surface of the water.

There were two long piers whose steel filigree work made spidery silhouettes against the sun-dazzle on the water a mile or two along and I turned right on to the bumpy surface of the minor road and drifted round following the curve of the bay, listening to a moody blues tune on the radio, the smoke from my cigarette chopped into segments by the breeze that was coming in the open window.

I was thinking about Cocos and all the things Prosser had told me yesterday and Stella's salty observations on the possibilities of the case. Such as they were. I smiled at the use of the adjective. Salty was the word all right out here. Today I just wanted to get the feel of Prosser's operations. Maybe I could get a line on the girl too from discreet inquiries around the bay. Maybe. We'd see.

I'd like to go out to Cocos some time too. That would be the place to begin serious inquiries. But there were obvious difficulties. The first was that it was guarded, with hard characters and dogs, according to Prosser. That might mean a trip by night if I wanted to find out anything. Then it would take five hours to get there.

So I'd have to stay somewhere or make my headquarters on one of Prosser's boats. I wasn't ready for that yet. There were a few other possible leads to pursue first. It might be better in fact if I drove on farther up the coast some time. I hadn't worked out the exact location but there was obviously a shorter sea crossing to Cocos that wouldn't take more than an hour or so. And it made far more sense than coming all the way from here.

Prosser said the place belonged to some millionaire. Stella had already been checking that but she hadn't come up with anything so far. I switched off the radio and wrestled on with a few points that were batting back and forth in what was left of my mind. I got over on to the shoulder half a mile short of the section I wanted and kept the motor running while I scanned the shore.

That didn't help very much and I eased back on to the road again, watching the silhouettes of the piers grow darker and more substantial as I got closer; noting the tangle of masts and rigging of the moored yachts; seeing now detail of the villas and solid stone-built houses rising from the hillside in back of the beach; one of them would undoubtedly belong to Prosser and maybe his brothers lived nearby.

There also looked to be a couple of restaurants and some shops; a small community clustering along the foreshore, with a definite flavour of its own. I noticed some more imposing buildings grouped around the yacht marina and the red-painted finger of concrete that jutted from the tangle of rocks outside the harbour entrance was certainly a lighthouse.

I'd already checked by the large-scale I had taped to the Buick dashboard and I was pretty certain it was Bridport Inlet; there was a strange configuration of the coast here with rocks jutting out from the sand but with a deep-water approach through the centre that led into a small, sheltered cove separated from the open bay. That was why there was a flashing light one side the channel and the lighthouse at the other, where the mass of rocks jutting out from the land penetrated into the main seaway.

A few moments later the white-painted board bearing the name of the hamlet showed up at the nearside road-edge. I tooled on down slowly, keeping my eyes on the rear-mirror in case I needed to warn overtaking traffic that I was turning off. There was nothing that close and I concentrated on a cluster of boat operations that were coming up on the offside of the road.

That was the beach-side, of course, where one would expect the boatyards to be; I gave my rear mirror a crooked grin as I pictured Stella's apposite comment on my reasoning. Or lack of it. The sun was hot on the back of my head and the sea-sparkle was beginning to tire the eyes. It was that sort of morning and even the breeze off the ocean wouldn't take the sting out the heat.

I checked my watch and saw it was just ten-thirty. I decided to stop at the nearest cafe I saw, get outside some coffee and maybe take in a little local gossip before I hit Prosser's place. It seemed like a good idea the more I thought about it. I was almost exactly halfway between the two big piers now; there was a mass of different craft rocking at anchor and the harsh cry of sea-birds that always begins to irritate if one stays in such places long. Leastways, it does in my case.

I saw Prosser's name in heavy black lettering on a board some twenty feet long that straddled the entrance to one of the biggest yards on the left-hand side the road. There was a cluster of smartly painted sheds down at the water's edge and the slow rumble of a marine diesel being run up in one of the buildings came across the sand toward me.

I drove on a couple of hundred yards to where blue and white flags were fluttering in back of a long boardwalk skirting the road. There was a restaurant sign in green neon and tables and chairs in white plastic set out on the ocean front verandah beneath blue canvas umbrellas. It looked cool and inviting and I turned the Buick quickly across the road on to the metalled car-park and killed the motor.

I got out the driving seat and slammed the door behind me, the sun hot and heavy on my head, the warm breeze seeming to sting the face. I got out my dark cheaters that made me look like Lee Marvin in one of his gentler moments and walked on over toward the café entrance, my shadow long and dark on the ground, my size nines making a faint scrunching noise in the sand. That was to be about the gentlest thing on the case I was getting into.

2

A tall girl with chestnut hair gathered into a pony tail came down the board-walk with long, leggy strides like she was on castors. She wore a red and white square print dress that I thought had gone out with Hollywood musicals and she was showing plenty of tanned cleavage that shot my morale to hell and back in this heat.

I ordered one of their big earthenware mugs of black coffee and a couple of Danish pastries to go with it. It was that sort of day. The girl herself was a lot like a Danish pastry come to think of it. She flushed slightly as she took my order like she could read my thoughts.

I sat back under one of the big blue umbrellas, the breeze cool on my face in here and admired her Swiss jewelled action all the way back to the restaurant entrance.

It took some little while to get my brain working again. There was something Stella had said last night that made sense. Not that that was anything unusual. She always made sense. It was to do with Prosser's boat, the one he usually took on fishing trips when he personally skippered tourists and people who needed to get from A to B. It was to do with Brown's expedition to Cocos and the reasons why the big man who'd fired at Prosser might have been there.

That aspect had puzzled me too. No

25

ordinary thief would blast away without trying to talk his way out. Though I could be on the wrong tack. L.A. was a very violent place nowadays; the whole world come to that. But it was worth looking into. And Stella had said I'd be freer if I gave the vessel the once-over myself without my style being cramped.

I knew the boat would be here because I'd made an arrangement with Prosser to come out today. But he'd suggested noon and I'd had no reason to quarrel with that. It was still short of eleven now and he had no idea I was already here.

Of course if the boat was out on a trip and wasn't due in until midday that was the end of it. But I figured it would be moored somewhere along the dock; or maybe out at one of the piers. It was worth a try and I had nothing to lose. The hot number was back now and she was giving me both barrels with her cleavage as she leaned over the table with my plate of pastries.

She had a little enamel badge clipped to the gingham costume over the left breast; it said Diane Morris and I pretended to admire it while she fiddled around with the coffee mug. She flushed again then though she didn't take the goodies away from under my chin. And I wasn't talking about the pastries. Not the Danish kind, anyway.

'Will there be anything else, sir?'

Her voice was low and sultry and any other

time I might have taken her up on the offer. But not this morning. I was here on business, and like I said it was too hot.

'I could think of a few things,' I said. 'Let's take a raincheck on it.'

She gave me about thirty-five millimetres' worth of teeth in her perfect smile.

'Perhaps you'd better have this.'

She slipped one of the restaurant pasteboards into my top pocket. I thanked her nicely and watched her all the way back to the main building. Diane Morris was certainly making a display of her nubility this morning. I didn't reach for the card but left it in my pocket. I knew it would contain a scribbled notation giving her name and private telephone number. So I didn't need to look. I'd done the same thing myself on the spur of the moment.

I turned my thoughts back to the case and the stuff on the table in front of me. I'd already settled with the Morris number and ten minutes later I got down off the verandah and went back along the boardwalk in the direction of Prosser's operation. I could see the tall, slim silhouette of the girl inside the restaurant. She appeared casual on the surface but I knew she was watching me all the way down the beach road until the cafe was hidden by a jink in the highway as I cut across the beach.

The sea-breeze was heavy and fresh on my

face and I could taste salt on my lips. One could get to like it out here. Though I knew I'd become bored with the routine after a few days. Ocean scenery isn't really my line. Some people become hooked on it but I found a certain monotony in seascapes, whatever the state of the weather. It was too much like the view from my office window. Though the passing show there was a little more animated.

I walked on across the soft sand, my feet crunching in its brittle, sugary mass, my shadow long and distorted on the ground. Prosser's boatyard was off to my left now as I was going down toward the beach where long, lazy lines of rollers were creaming in among the minute figures of the swimmers. I was making for the nearest pier, that closest to the lighthouse that guarded the approach to Bridport Inlet.

Like I figured, when I got up closer to it, I found there were a number of sets of heavy wooden steps piled into the side of the steel latticework of the pier itself that were obviously used by fishermen and tourists to gain access to the beach.

I got up top and found the pier was an all-metal construction, with slatted plates bolted to the main structure that made a hollow clanking noise under my tread. There were a few people strolling on the pier farther out and rather more fishermen whose poles were dangling optimistically into the disturbed

28

water on the lee side.

I looked back toward the shore where the flags of Prosser's boatyard fluttered. I was about a hundred feet or more out here and I couldn't see anybody around. I turned back toward the seaward end of the pier and plugged on down. I was about a dozen yards from the water still and I guessed the bay was pretty shallow farther in.

I could see the deep grooves in the sand at the shoreward side where vessels were winched up and I noticed by the seaweed and red kelp adhering to the piles of the pier that the tide was a fair way out now. I was above the water and I paused opposite a large metal sponson that jutted out over the ocean, admiring the cast a tall, red-faced character in a green jersey was making. The float hit the water almost without a ripple and the green eyes that matched the sea twinkled with satisfaction beneath the white floppy hat.

I walked on then, knowing I'd have to descend a wooden ladder on the choppy, offshore side of the pier if I wanted to board the *Glory B*. Assuming she was here, of course.

It took me some time but I spotted her in the end, tied up to the pier ladder, protected by pudding fenders, among a mass of other craft. There was no-one around on the decks but I spent a little while surveying the scene. I had a good view from here because the moored craft were a little way down but I knew there'd be people about because ropes and tow-lines would have to be slacked off as the tide continued falling. Or tightened if it was coming in.

The *Glory B* was a large, sea-going outfit with stainless steel rails and a blue hull; there were two steel chairs for marlin fishing fixed in the stern with fittings for more, and a lot of other gear which I was too idle to register for the moment. That the *Glory B* was here meant that she was maybe due to take off later in the day.

There was no future in hanging around here so I went down the nearest ladder hand over hand, the sun hot on my head and shoulders, the sound of the sea loud and insistent now that I was below the level of the pier decking. I had no business here, of course, though I knew Prosser wouldn't mind.

But if there were fishermen or other people about they wouldn't know what craft I was bound for. I couldn't see anyone around and it was a little tricky gauging the fall of the tide when I swung down from the ladder on to the deck planking of a big gaff-rigged sailboat. I went across the adjoining decks quickly and up the short teak ladder on to the welldeck of the *Glory B*.

The cabin was amidships like one would expect it to be, with a large teak door held by a steel bolt with a facility for a securing pin and padlock; and a sliding coachroof up above. It was abaft the wheelhouse which was high up like all these tubs. I went over to the cabin entrance, noting that the shaft of the bolt could be completely slid out of its fitting.

That was for night-time so that people inside the cabin, who'd secure the door from the interior, couldn't be locked in by an intruder. It had happened before while thieves ransacked the wheelhouse of all its valuable electronic equipment in a number of instances up and down the coast.

I remembered what Prosser had said the previous day and took my time examining the edge of the door and the hatchway above. Someone had first tried to jemmy back the hatchway but that would have been impossible as the massive teak coachroof moved in equally sturdy metal runners.

The man with the jemmy had then tried the padlock area because there were big grooves scored in the teak surround and fine scratches on the lock-plate, like Prosser had said. There was nothing else to be found here, except confirmation of my client's story and I'd expected that anyway.

I slid the door back. It folded in two, like all those doors do, and when secured it would have been further reinforced by a couple of bolts on the inside; to pin the wings in position. The companionway smelt fresh and salty with the faint aroma of cooking that emanated from the small galley on the

31

starboard side.

I padded on down the short corridor to the saloon which had a teak door too, but with glass in the top panels. The cabin was pretty roomy for a craft this size, with leather-cushioned seating and a gimballed table in the centre. There were a lot of books; mostly navigational aids and chart volumes in shelves on either side; and a strong smell of cigar smoke now that I was in here.

I went down the saloon slowly, reaching out to take the odd volume down from time to time, my ears attuned to the creaking and thumping noises the vessel was making as it moved to the heavy ocean swell; bumping occasionally against the fenders between the hull and the pier timbers.

I was bent over the cushions, my head halfway in an open locker, trying to make out the contents of the shadowy interior when another door in the bulkhead behind me opened and something only slightly less heavy than the Queen Mary fell on me. The next second I was fighting for my life.

CHAPTER FOUR

1

My face was ground heavily into the leather cushions and the big hand at the back of my neck shifted its grip and started slamming my skull against the locker door. I saw the red light of Very flares against the darkness and then I'd rammed my elbow back in a reflexive action, finding soft stomach tissue.

The man who was doing such a good job of demolishing my ego gave an explosive grunt and the fingers at my neck faltered and fell away. I pushed back from the banquette with all my force, feeling the heavy but out of condition body of my attacker sag.

I got some more elbow work in, heard grunts of pain then; the big, dark-haired man in the blue nautical blazer somersaulted over the table, setting the overhead lamp swinging and making jars and bottles on the locker shelves jump and rattle as he crashed into the doors.

I'd taken off my dark cheaters before I'd come in here but the man whose face was distorted with rage still wore his; one lens had cracked where he'd caught it somewhere and he looked like a wounded insect as he lunged at me again. I was ready for him this time and

33

I sidestepped, catching my knee against one of the heavy wooden uprights of the bench on my side the cabin.

I felt a stabbing pain and doubled over, missing the heavy metal teapot that dark glasses had thrown. It sailed over my head and bounced among the books on the shelves. I was still off balance when the big man's flailing right, aimed nowhere in particular, caught me across the ear and sent me up against the wooden bulkhead.

I felt my lip split and tasted salt blood on my mouth. I was angry then for the first time this afternoon and dropped quickly to the deck. The man in the blue blazer was too impulsive; his head and shoulders crashed against the lockers in his bull rush.

He grunted again and went down in a tangle of books and expensive-looking nautical equipment. I crawled away, my leg still throbbing, fighting waves of nausea. I guessed my brain was a little addled from the blows on the ear and head. Prosser's case was beginning to yield results. If it was going to be this rough I'd better start carrying the Smith-Wesson.

I wished I had it along this morning. It would have saved a lot of physical punishment on both sides. The man in the blue blazer was up now, blood trickling from a cut above the hairline. He wasn't pretty before; now he looked like a battle casualty from *Gone With the Wind*.

'Can't we talk this over?' I said.

I was up too, able to use my leg, the waves of pain receding. The man in the dark cheaters gave an animal snarl and came at me once more. I chopped him in the neck and got a good left into the jaw. Though he was out of condition he was pretty tough and he tried a bear hug. While he was thinking about it I broke his hold and we both fell back to the deck, swapping punches as we rolled over.

They were only glancing blows so far as I was concerned but my head was muzzy and the scene started to recede; I got a good one into his gut and he sobbed for breath, falling over into the far side of the cabin. But he had his hand in a corner cupboard whose door was open and he came up with a rain of objects which I had to ward off.

There was a metal bowl; a pudding fender; and a blunt kitchen knife among them. The air seemed to be full of gear, like that famous photo Dali made some time during the war, and I was kept busy crouching below the table edge, the crashes and bangings the fusillade stirred making the cabin seem like something out of a D-Day newsreel.

I was getting tired of this and when there came a break in the barrage I went over the top of the table in a long dive; I landed square on the belly of the man with dark glasses and his breath went out with an expiring sound. I slammed his head into the heavy wooden

35

cupboard then and he passed out cold. I got up feeling old and weary and full of no coffee.

The blood on my tongue tasted fresher and saltier and I caught a glimpse of my reflection in a small circular mirror screwed to the far bulkhead. I looked like I felt and turned away quickly. I was still standing there, re-knotting my tie and running my hand through my hair when there was a sudden draught on my back.

'Jeezechrise!' said the enormous man who filled the entire doorway.

He looked from me to the character in the dark cheaters and then back again.

'You mind telling me what the hell's going on?' Alex Prosser said.

2

There was humour in the big man's eyes now. He lifted the groaning figure of the character in dark cheaters like he was a rag doll and no weight at all. He sat him back on the cushions of the starboard bench and stared at him thoughtfully.

'This here's my brother,' he said. 'Guess he thought you were an intruder come back. Maybe the guy with the heater.'

My astonishment must have shown on my face because Prosser gave a sudden bellowing laugh that made the cabin reverberate.

'I'm sorry,' I said. 'He jumped me suddenly. I had to defend myself.'

Prosser nodded his head portentously. Today he wore a lightweight blue sweater and faded blue jeans that made him look more enormous than ever.

'Don't blame yourself, Mr Faraday.'

He grinned.

'Leastways, it proves you can handle yourself. My brother's been a middle-weight champion in his time. Amateur, of course.'

'Of course,' I said.

I sat down on the bench opposite. My body was developing all kinds of aches and I felt tired to hell. As well as embarrassed. But both would pass.

'I'll apologise to him if it would do any good,' I said.

Prosser glanced at the recumbent figure of his brother.

'When he comes around,' he said absently.

He fished in one of the lockers, came up with a bottle and some glasses.

'I got in an hour early,' I said. 'I figured you might be busy so I came out on the pier for a stroll. I spotted the *Glory B* and thought I'd give her the onceover. I'd just got in the cabin when half a house fell on me.'

Prosser paused in his pouring, licked his lips reflectively.

'Lionel always was an impetuous type,' he said. 'He could simply have asked you what you were doing. But that's not his style. He always jumps in with two feet. He handles the

37

engineering side.'

I passed my hand across my jaw. It wasn't broken, like I'd figured at first. I took the glass from Prosser. The contents tasted fiery and good. I felt energy creeping back into my limbs.

'How come you didn't hear the ruckus?' I said.

Prosser shrugged, sitting down opposite with his own glass, ignoring the sprawled form of his brother.

'I was up checking the forward bilges,' he said. 'You can't hear much there, what with the confined space and the slap of the water. I was just coming aft because I noticed it was near the time of your arrival.'

He looked at me shrewdly.

'You find anything of interest?'

I shook my head.

'I examined the hatch. It confirmed what you already told me. I didn't have time for anything else before your brother jumped me.'

Prosser spread his hands wide.

'Be my guest. You want to look around now?'

I shook my head again, regretted it; feeling the front of my face might fall off.

'I think I've seen enough for one morning. Shall we go back to your yard? There's a number of things I'd like to discuss. After we've finished our drinks, of course.'

Prosser took the hint, slid the bottle over

toward me. I re-filled my glass and toasted him in silence.

'What about your brother?' I said.

Prosser grunted. He took the dark cheaters off Lionel Prosser's face, slid up his right eyelid and examined the eyeball intently. He appeared satisfied because he soon finished his Dr Kildare act and put the glasses back on over the closed eyes.

The cracked lens of the cheaters came into focus briefly and I remembered then what it had reminded me of in the middle of our session swapping punches; that famous still from the *Battleship Potemkin*. Not that it helped Prosser's case at all. But it proved my brain was still functioning.

'He'll be around in a couple of minutes,' he said. 'You can apologise then.'

He drained his glass, reached out for the bottle.

'We'll go up to my house in a little while, Mike. You can wash up there and I'll introduce you to my family. It will be more private for talking. And I've got lunch laid on. I thought you'd like that.'

I raised my glass in salute again.

'Sounds just fine,' I said.

CHAPTER FIVE

1

'No hard feelings, then?' I said.

Lionel Prosser gave me an insincere smile. Alex Prosser grinned broadly over his brother's head.

'My fault, Mr Faraday, for flying off the handle.'

I felt my jaw again.

'You pack a mean wallop, Mr Prosser.'

Lionel Prosser smiled genuinely this time. He had a couple of deep, yellowish-black bruises on either cheek that made him look like one of those pierrots one used to see in one's childhood; and he'd replaced his dark cheaters with a new pair. He looked almost as good as new. Which was more than I could say for myself. I'd tidied myself up in Prosser's bathroom but I was avoiding mirrors for the time being.

'Like I said he's been a boxer,' Alex Prosser said proprietorially. 'He's the engineering expert in the family.'

He looked thoughtfully out the big picture window of his study, which faced the Pacific; the boatyard buildings could be vaguely seen below, screened by flowering shrubs at the end of the patio. We'd come straight up here to this big, pleasant, stone-built house that looked well equipped to face both the rigours of winter gales that sometimes whip the coast; and the scorching heat of summer.

'I'm sorry you won't be able to meet my other brother, Mike. He's the accountant I've been telling you about.'

'It doesn't matter,' I said. 'Two's enough for one day.'

Even Lionel Prosser joined in the big man's laugh. I sipped at my tulip-shaped glass of chilled white wine, conscious that the throbbing in my temples had receded, only vaguely aware of my surroundings. What was left of my brain was still recycling possibilities. About the case, of course. Such as it was. And I still had to face Stella over this morning's debacle. I could imagine her expression.

'Have you any more ideas about this man Brown?' I said.

The two brothers exchanged glances. Lionel Prosser sipped at his whisky and soda. I noticed then that the breast pocket of his otherwise immaculate blazer had been torn, one side hanging by the final threads. It had been quite a fracas while it lasted.

Lionel Prosser shrugged.

'I never saw the man, Mr Faraday. That's not really my department. I rarely see the people who charter our craft. I'm strictly a backroom merchant.'

'But you must have some ideas,' I persisted.

He twisted up his lips. With the two pierrot-type bruises it didn't make him look any more personable.

'I discussed it with Alex, of course, on several occasions. It seemed that his business out at Cocos may not have been legal. Especially now that his body has been found. But it wasn't our affair.'

He gave me a sharp glance from behind the new pair of cheaters.

'We never inquire into our clients' motives, Mr Faraday.'

I took another sip at my wine. I was growing more mellow by the minute.

'Not even when it's illegal?' I said.

Dark flushes were spreading across the younger Prosser's cheeks now.

'That's an unfair remark and uncalled-for, Mr Faraday.'

I gave him one of my best twisted grins.

'I'll withdraw it, then. Or, as the legal boys say, re-phrase the question. What did you think he might have been up to out at Cocos? It may be some help to me in going at this tangle.'

Alex Prosser was smiling at me approvingly now. I guessed that maybe the brothers had a little friction from time to time. But that was none of my business.

'I'll think about it, Mr Faraday, and let you know after lunch,' Lionel Prosser said enigmatically. 'You'll want to see round the yard and the installations, of course.'

42

'Sure,' I said. 'Now that I'm here. I'll have a lot of questions to ask.'

Alex Prosser nodded his massive head.

'That's fine, Mike. We'll both be available.'

He looked at the watch clamped round his tremendous wrist with what looked like cast-off cable from some ocean-going liner.

'I have a short hire-trip at five o'clock. But I can give you all the time in the world until then.'

'We'll get to it,' I promised him.

We were interrupted by the study door opening and Prosser's wife, a tall, vivacious-looking woman in her early forties, with gleaming dark hair, glanced in inquiringly.

'Lunch is ready, gentlemen, any time you require it,' she said briskly.

Alex Prosser got up with a vaguely menacing movement. He looked at me approvingly, draining the last of his wine.

'We're more than ready, Dolores.'

2

'What do you think, Mr Faraday?' Prosser said for the third time in the past half hour.

I shrugged.

'It's far too early, Alex. I'm mulling a few ideas around in my mind.'

It was past three now. We'd had a great lunch and I'd drunk rather too much of a good red than was suitable for the temperature this afternoon. But I'd sweat that out in the next

43

hour. The past had been spent in touring the boatyard and workshops. Lionel Prosser had excused himself and gone off sourly to his own office.

Like I figured he hadn't come up with any interesting ideas. I didn't blame him for what had happened. Except that he shouldn't have jumped the gun like that. Fortunately his wife hadn't shown for lunch or it could have been embarrassing. For me, that is. Though Alex Prosser's wife had seemed amused at her brother-in-law's battered condition. I'd guessed then they maybe didn't hit it off too well.

We'd talked a lot about the situation over lunch. It hadn't helped. The elder Prosser had gotten a lot off his chest. He was still feeling the after-effects of a near blasting the night he'd found the prowler aboard the *Glory B*, so it probably did him good to purge it from his system. I hadn't figured any brilliant theories either, during the conversation or on the tour of the yards that followed.

I was impressed with the scale of the operation. But that didn't help me any over my client's problem. We still had three disparate segments that might or might not be connected. An obvious mobster hired Prosser to take him out to Cocos Island. Prosser is given the brush on his return and never sees the unlikely named Brown again. Except for a picture in a newspaper cutting when his bullet-ridden corpse is washed up on shore. Segment one.

Segment two. A blonde girl is inquiring after Brown at Prosser's boatyard. Before Brown is washed up, obviously. In all senses of the word. That could be important. Or not. Whichever way one looked at it. The girl and Brown could be connected. Or maybe the girl was acting as a front for some people who wanted to get Brown.

But in that case why did a gunman try to break into Prosser's sea-going cruiser? That was an open question and there was no sense in my trying to beat my brains out over it on such a hot afternoon. We'd come to a halt at one of the slipways now where a sizeable sea-going yacht, built in the yard to the Prosser Brothers' own designs, was nearing completion. I guessed she'd be going down the slip any day.

The tide was almost in now and all the piles of the pier were awash; the edge of the surf-line came almost within yards of the end of the slipway. Even so it had to run a long way out. I guessed then that Prosser had one of the prime positions out here. On the far side of the two piers, way up the coast, the bay and the coastal waters were much more unprotected and at the mercy of wind and sea when it blew up hard.

Thank you, Long John Silver, I told myself. I'd sensed the disappointment in Prosser's voice a few moments ago and now I turned back to him. The big red-faced man, who'd changed into duck trousers and a crumpled open-neck shirt was standing at the end of the slipway, rooting in a pile of wood-shavings with the toe of his heavy boot.

The air was full of good smells; the aromatic scent of newly planed wood; tar; and over all the slightly astringent salt air of the sea.

'You mustn't expect too much first time around, Alex,' I said. 'I've only been a few hours on the case.'

Prosser shot me a downbeat smile.

'Sure, Mike. I guess I was expecting too much. Sure as hell Mr Holmes himself couldn't have picked up much out here this afternoon.'

I didn't answer for a moment, my eyes shaded against the sun on the water, as I looked at the long, black silhouettes of the strings of walkers who were perambulating to and from the nearest pier.

'What's with your brother?' I said. 'You don't get on very well?'

It may have been my imagination but I fancied his face grew even redder.

'We get on well enough. But you got to understand him. He's a difficult man in some ways.'

'It seemed to me your wife wasn't too fond of him at lunch,' I said.

Prosser gave me a battered smile.

'You have a point there, Mike. But then you know what wives are. They've had a few family spats from time to time. But Dolores has come to terms with him. Every family has small problems like that.'

'I'll take your word for it,' I said. 'What about your hire?'

Prosser shot a glance at his wrist-watch that had a face like a town hall clock.

'I still got best part of an hour if there's anything else you want to see.'

'I haven't been in those sheds over there,' I said.

A worried look passed over Prosser's big, amiable face.

'We don't normally show visitors around there, Mike. It's kinda restricted.'

'In what way?' I said.

Prosser hesitated, then came closer, lowering his voice though his nearest employee was twenty yards away, painting the hull of a sloop; and a speedboat was making a hell of a racket half a mile from shore.

'I guess it'll be all right to show you, Mike, but don't tell anyone about it.'

'I don't get it,' I said.

Prosser led the way across the concrete yard to the big silver-painted metal sheds in the distance.

'It's a sort of defence contract, Mike. I'm not being pretentious. We build vessels for the Coastguard and other official bodies from time

47

to time. They have weapons, radar, advanced electronic equipment; that sort of thing. The people working on them have to sign agreements on confidentiality. It's all bull, of course.'

'Of course,' I said. 'You don't think the character trying to break into the *Glory B* could have been after something like that?'

'It's unlikely, Mike,' Prosser said. 'We don't keep papers on such matters aboard our boats. Besides, if anyone was after valuable electronic gear they'd break into the boat-sheds, wouldn't they?'

'You're right,' I said. 'It was just a hunch.'

I stared at Prosser. The big man had suddenly stopped in his tracks like someone had put a right into his gut. He grasped my arm with a power that momentarily made me flinch.

'That's her, Mike!' he said in a hoarse whisper.

I looked in the direction he was pointing, saw a sudden flash of red against the background of moving cars along the beach road that passed the yard.

'I'll buy it,' I said.

I couldn't keep the irritation out my voice and Prosser shot me a reproachful glance.

'I'm certain of it, Mike. She's even wearing the same outfit. It's the blonde girl! Miss Green. The one who was inquiring after the guy whose body was fished out the bay.'

The rest of his words were chopped off by the breeze. I was already halfway across the yard, making for the entrance, the ache in my leg forgotten.

CHAPTER SIX

1

I pounded on down the beach road in the heat and the dust, the snarl of motors from passing traffic adding to the jumble of my thoughts. Somewhere ahead, among the pedestrians and the swirl of children in swim-suits pattering from cola-stall to fudge concession the splash of scarlet made a bright, bobbing bead that gave me my heading.

Fortunately, the girl was going in the direction I'd stashed the Buick. I could see she had long blonde hair now and what I could make out of her figure was all right. The splash of red was a silk blouse and below it she wore white linen trousers that hugged her figure.

She was going at quite a lick; almost running in fact and I had a job to keep up. I wondered if she had been hanging around Prosser's place. It was possible. But then again why make herself so conspicuous. The scarlet shirt or blouse stood out a long way away. Though a lot of people out here at the beach were just as brightly dressed. I hoped Prosser's eyesight was good. After all, he'd only caught a glimpse of the girl as she passed the yard entrance. Then I remembered that most sailors had excellent eyesight. And in the short time I'd known him I hadn't seen Alex Prosser using glasses.

I had shortened the distance and I was about a hundred yards from where I'd parked the Buick. I now had a problem. Either the girl was taking a stroll along the beach road, perhaps with a view to visiting someone, or she had her own heap somewhere along here. I had to decide whether to continue on foot or get behind the wheel of the Buick. Either way I still had difficulties. If I walked too far along the shoreline and she then got into a car I would blow it.

On the other hand if I picked up the Buick now I'd have to get in the traffic stream, which had considerably thickened up since this morning. Which meant I couldn't shadow her at walking pace without causing a monumental jam. And even without the rest of the traffic to contend with I'd certainly cause a lot of comment out here by driving my heap behind the girl at a steady five miles an hour.

I gave myself one of my sardonic looks as I glimpsed my reflection in the window of a beach kiosk I was just passing. The girl had slackened her pace a little and was looking aimlessly about her, but I still couldn't get a proper view of her face. There was just the shoulder-length hair, on which the sun struck warming glints; the red silk shirt—I could see it was a shirt now—and the white trousers.

She was pretty tall and she looked, for one brief moment, as she put up her hand to draw the hair back from her eyes, as if she wore some sort of gold bangle round her right wrist. It wasn't much to go on but any little detail might help if I lost her out here this afternoon. Which looked extremely likely as we'd just passed the Buick and I might soon be out of reach if I didn't make up my mind soon.

My tiredness was falling away from me though the exercise was giving me stomach gas with all the wine I'd drunk at lunch. It sure is one hell of a life being a P.I., Mike, I told myself. The girl had stopped, examining the magazines on a portable news-stand and I stopped too, looking out to sea like I was intensely interested in the result of a dinghy race whose contestants were just fetching up round the nearest marker.

With my facial bruises I probably looked like a badly blocked-in copy of The Boyhood of Raleigh. Or something about that price-range. When I turned back the girl was buying some magazine with a three-colour cover and rummaging for change in the brown leather shoulder-bag she carried.

I was standing about halfway between her and the Buick, which was behind me, of course. I had about 50 yards to go either way. The girl was still hesitating and sorting her change. Then she paid for the magazine, still without turning in my direction, and walked quickly into a parking lot that was set back beneath the low cliff the far side of the coast road.

I went back to the Buick, feeling anonymous and private beneath my dark cheaters. The Buick was facing up toward Prosser's place so I turned on to the road-edge and reversed, keeping an anxious eye on the rear mirror. The heat from the cushions was throwing rivulets of perspiration off me to add to the pleasure and I opened the windows when I had a free hand.

I was edging slowly toward the news-stand now, still keeping on the verge. There was nothing in front of me here and no-one walking up from the beach. I had an anxious moment or two because there were three vehicles coming out from the parking lot opposite.

There was an elderly man with a black mustache driving a beige Packard and no sign of the girl; no passenger even. The second vehicle, a big black saloon had sun dazzle on the windows, which made it impossible to see the interior, so it obviously had air-conditioning. My nerves were a little jittery when I spotted the girl driving a white open sport two-seater, her hair streaming in the breeze as she gunned up behind the saloon. I kept my eye on the rear-mirror, waiting until the big fruit-truck had passed, before I edged out and crossed the road to the correct lane.

I was just in time to see the white sport job slot in behind the saloon. Both vehicles went away fast, going in the direction of Santa Barbara. I settled down to follow.

2

The girl drove on a couple of miles on the curving beach-road before she slotted right up a winding secondary lane back from the beach. There were a couple of private cars in between us now and I was content to leave it like that. At first I'd figured the people in the saloon were connected with the girl in some way but they went straight on at the intersection and disappeared in the heat haze that was coming up.

I settled down then and concentrated on the white sport job. The girl certainly knew how to drive. She had plenty of power under the bonnet but she had a light hand on the steering and an equally light foot on the accelerator pedal. Which doesn't always follow. The road wound upward and I steered with one hand and lit a cigarette with the other, feathering out blue smoke through the open driving windows.

It was late afternoon now but the sun still had a stinging, antiseptic quality and the light through the trees made deep bars of shadow on the dusty road which had a tiring, strobing effect on the eyes. The girl eased up at a set of traffic lights where the side lane met the inner coastal highway.

She went straight across when the lights changed, up a narrow canyon road opposite, one of the two vehicles between us turning left. That still left one but I dropped back a little then as I didn't want the Buick to appear too conspicuous. Not that the girl would have any reason to think she might be followed.

For all I knew her inquiries at Prosser's boatyard might have been quite innocuous. It seemed, on the surface, that the man known as Brown might have been a mobster. Prosser had spotted the gun-bulge in his coat. But supposing he had been on the side of the law and the people on Cocos had him taken out. In which case the girl could be an associate. Or maybe a reporter on the scent of a story.

I screwed up my face in the rear mirror in what was meant to be a wry grimace but which came out as something strictly from an old Karloff movie. The bruises on my face were a treat now. I'd momentarily forgotten until the pain in my jaw returned. There was an even worse possibility that I hadn't gone into. That Prosser was entirely mistaken and that this girl had nothing whatsoever to do with the number who'd turned up at his yard.

All blondes look alike; superficially at least. But Prosser had seen her close up and spoken to her. He ought to know. I thrust the factor that he might be wrong to one side and blotted

55

it out with a news bulletin on the radio. It passed the time and killed the nagging doubts at the back of what was laughingly called my mind.

The white sport job went on, winding upward between steep shoulders of rock as we rose higher in the foothills. I could see snow on the top of Mount Baldy from far off and behind us the broad shield of the Pacific, emerald-green shading to dark indigo was mottled with the rusty red of floating kelp beds.

The beige Packard in front of me signalled right presently and turned into a winding driveway. The girl went straight on and I dropped back again, letting her get around the next bend each time, like I wasn't interested at all. I was beginning to think I was on a useless chase when the sport job signalled right too and the girl turned off on to a small canyon road.

I throttled back and gave her time to get well in and then pulled on to the rocky shoulder of the road and killed the motor. The soft sighing of the breeze and the cries of birds filtered back in and I got out the Buick, closing the door softly, grateful for the coolness of the air on my face. I went on cautiously to the mouth of the lane, my feet gritting with a sharp brittle sound on the fragments of rock underfoot. A couple of cars passed, going in opposite directions but traffic was thin up

56

here.

There was no sign of the girl's heap but there was a white notice board set back a couple of yards from the road saying it was a private lane and giving the names of the houses. There were six in all and I hoped they wouldn't be too far down because I intended to walk from here on in. It was too conspicuous to use the Buick and the sound of its motor could have been heard a mile away.

I'd only gone a couple of hundred yards, turning a shallow curve before the first two houses showed; almost opposite each other on the far sides of the road. There was no sign of the girl's car and for a moment I had an uneasy feeling that she might have driven right through.

Then another sign indicated that the place was a cul-de-sac. I breathed again. I'd had plenty of wasted afternoons in my life but this was one I didn't want to waste. Especially as it was the only lead we had so far. I'd like to report something reassuring to Prosser when I got back.

I went on again, walking on scrubland at the road-edge that was burnt almost black with the sun. Even through the dark cheaters the glare was uncomfortable on the eyes and sweat was trickling down my neck to make a damp, sticky patch in the small of my back.

I got round the second curve in the road and found a big split-level bungalow built of the local stone; with a green-tile roof; set back behind a high stone wall; and with the grounds laid out like rockeries; with cactus plants and palms and other stuff that flourished in the arid, stony soil up here.

There was a bright blue Mercedes sitting out front, making a nice sun-glitter, facing down the drive toward me. The heavy iron gates to the drive were wide open and pegged back and I could see the white sport job standing near the Mercedes. The girl had driven around a huge circular rockery crowned with palms that sat in the centre of the driveway fronting the house and made a turn for cars so they wouldn't have to reverse when coming away.

I got on the opposite side of the road, in the shadow of undergrowth and walked on past as quickly as possible, hoping I hadn't been spotted. Pedestrians up here must be as rare as virgins in Beverly Hills. My leg was hurting again now. I went on down, conscious of a faint ache in my arches too. It was the first sign of age in a P.I. and I wondered how soon it would be before Stella had to push me to cases in my wheel-chair.

The joke lasted me all the time it took me to pad around the perimeter of the bungalow grounds. The wall petered out presently in a shoulder of hillside and I crossed the road, making sure I wasn't overlooked by any other houses. There was a small canyon here, which

58

was crossed by a heavy metal bridge so I guessed some of the other properties were down there.

I went up a rocky slope that was heavy with scrub oaks, lizards and bird-song and I found I could jump over a low fence at the side of the property. I worked my way through the trees feeling hot, dusty and in need of an iced beer. The bungalow was side on to me now and I threaded down through the grounds, hardly noticing the detail, though I could see a big swimpool up on a terrace.

There was no-one around unless one counted some half dozen torpid carp which paddled flaccidly around a big ornamental pool that had been blasted from the rock, keeping in the shade of the trees. The expression of the nearest reminded me of Lionel Prosser's face when I'd finally outed him.

I went up a set of zig-zag stone steps that wound around the contours of the hillside, making for the side of the house. There was a fancy flagged path here and I followed it, keeping in the shadow as much as possible, conscious of the stifling heat that the trees and the underbrush were absorbing from the house façade.

I rounded the corner on to the terrace, stopping by a set of big French doors that gave on to some large rooms because they were repeated quite a long way across the façade.

The shadows of branches were sharp-edged on the white walls of the house and the wind made odd scraping noises as it pushed foliage against the tiles somewhere.

I was still standing there, listening to the heavy beating of my heart when I heard the girl scream from somewhere inside the house. It was a high, insistent scream like she was in fear of her life and it fuelled my reactions like nothing else could have done.

I got a short run in and put my shoulder at the French doors, going through into the room beyond in a shower of glass and broken timber that would have made James Cagney proud of me.

3

I went down on one knee in the room interior, blinking at the contrast between the dim light in here and the glare of sun outside. I skidded against a padded leather chair and carried on across the parquet, reaching for my shoulder-holster and the Smith-Wesson that wasn't there.

The girl with the long fair hair who was half-crouched on the divan and the big man with the hard face who stood with his fist balled above her remained as though cast in bronze for a brief fraction of time. In that moment I took in the long room got up as a library; the sheeted furniture and the half-empty crates of books scattered around.

I guessed then that the place had been rented furnished and that the big man wouldn't be the owner. That and a dozen other thoughts were pin-balling through my mind as I went on skittering across toward the far wall. The girl had a thin smear of blood on her face and there was desperation in her eyes as she twisted her head to stare disbelievingly at me.

The big man's reaction was a little slow but then he'd been busy in other directions when I came in. He made an ugly sound, his big yellow teeth like a wolf's in the dark gash of his mouth. He clawed at the inside of his jacket. I was across the floor now and my hand was already round the neck of the big painted vase. I hoped it wasn't a Ming.

My aim was good, my reflexes operating pretty well. The vase caught him a heavy blow across the shoulder. It also caught his outstretched fingers before it shattered on the wall, extracting a grunt of pain. But he still hadn't drawn the piece before I was up and launching myself through the air. It's all action today, Mike, I told myself.

The girl wriggled aside and my balled hands caught the big man in the midriff before he could get to his inside pocket. His breath went out in a long, explosive sound and then we were going over the divan. The girl had writhed away like a snake. I hoped she hadn't got a gun too. And that she was on my side.

She wasn't with the big man, that was for sure. I didn't know whether there was anyone else in the house but I was pinning my hopes on the two being alone. There were only two cars outside. I didn't have time to see what the girl was doing because the big man was in an ugly mood and was flailing at my face. I had his right wrist pinned; he was pretty strong but I thought I could handle him in a rough-house.

And this was likely to be as rough as they come. He was still reaching inside his jacket with his free hand when I got a good left into his throat. It was aimed at his jaw but he'd wriggled aside and the blow went low. He made another gurgling noise and his hand fell away from his pocket, chopping at me.

In the brief respite I could see the girl crawling around among the debris on the floor. I thought she was doing something important until I saw she was only looking for her shoulder bag. It had slipped open, its contents scattered on the floor. Any other time it would have been funny. But not this afternoon.

'You might help,' I said, as the big man's left hand came over and caught me by the lapels. I could hear muscles creaking as we both shifted grip. The girl didn't say anything; her green eyes looked at me incuriously. I guessed she was probably in shock. To be slapped around by the six-footer I was swapping punches with was no joke for me. To a girl it was something else again.

The big man moved suddenly then, took me by surprise, his knee in my stomach. I went over backward, missing the girl, slid across the parquet again. I picked up a heavy teak coffee table, charged back. I was halfway through my dive, using the table as a battering ram when the big man got the pistol out.

It was so big it looked like a Colt. The heavy edge of the teak forced up his gun hand, rammed it under his chin. His head snapped back and the thunder of the explosion split the room apart as fragments of wood and plaster rained from the ceiling, making a grey mist in here through which the girl still groped unsteadily.

It looked like something out of a surrealist movie but I had no time for the finer points of the action. The big man went over at a terrific speed, smashing in the front of a glass bureau. But he still had the Colt and I went after him, pinning his gun hand.

His eyes had an insane glare now and there were ugly white patches round his mouth. Foam didn't actually come out his lips but I felt it might. I slammed his arm back two or three times against the glass door of the bookcase, felt it crack but the big guy had a grip like steel. He fired again while I was doing that and strips of parquet whirled about the room.

The girl was doing some more aerobic exercises on the floor, but I had no leisure to admire them. The man in the dark suit was trying to make me slacken my grip but I wasn't having any. It was the easiest way to commit suicide and I aimed to be around when the champagne corks popped in the twenty-first century. With a little luck that is.

His third shot hit the floor between us, the ricochet sending divan cushion feathers flying. The girl took a hand then. She came between us and hit the big man between the eyes as hard as she could with a steel poker she'd picked up from somewhere. His pupils glazed and he sagged; I felt his fingers slacken on the trigger and had the pistol half in my grasp when the girl overdid things.

She brought the poker back to deliver another blow and caught me across the side of the face. The scene blurred considerably but I still had the sense to keep hold of the pistol. I tore it out the big man's grasp as I went back on to the floor.

'Thanks a lot,' I told the blonde number.

While I was toying with the desire to lie down and sleep for a couple of hours there was a scrabbling on the floor and a door slammed somewhere up the far end of the room. I started to claw myself up as the Mercedes gunned along the front of the house and went away very fast, taking a pound or two of rubber off the tyres.

I must have really passed out then because when the scene focused up again I was lying on the splintered parquet, the pistol still beneath my outstretched hand, the girl just going out the shattered French window on to the terrace. She glanced back once and I'd like to be able to say there was compassion and concern in the deep green eyes but I'd only be fooling myself.

I made myself comfortable after that, listening to the faint hum of the girl's heap receding into the far distance. I had all the time in the world now. I only hoped the real owners of the house wouldn't show before I'd had a good rest and cleaned myself up.

It was principally mirrors I was worried about. What I might see there. Before, I'd looked like Karloff in makeup for *Frankenstein*. Now I was likely to be starring in a sub-standard sequel. Like *The Monster Returns*. I made sure I had no broken bones before resting up a little while longer.

It was about five when I woke and quit the set for World War Three. I found a cloakroom on the ground floor and washed-up, avoiding my image in the mirror. There was no-one around when I left the house, the sun hot and heavy on my head, the big man's pistol hard against my aching chest muscles. I could check out the ownership but I knew there'd be no way of tracing it. Pros always buy their pieces for specific jobs; they never use properly registered weapons.

I drove back in to L.A. without hitting Prosser's place. There was no point now. I'd phone him this evening and give him a report. Right now I wanted a shower, a good steak and a cool beer.

Tomorrow I'd discuss things with Stella and give my brain cells another shaking up. It seemed like a long way back in to Park West.

CHAPTER SEVEN

1

'So you blew it?' Stella said.

'You could say that,' I admitted modestly.

'I do say it,' Stella said crisply.

She stood over me at the desk and did soothing things with styptic pencils and little pieces of invisible plaster. By the time she'd finished I'd only look like an extra in *Son of Frankenstein* instead of the star.

She stopped at last and put a cool hand on my forehead. Her fingers rested there just a little bit longer than was necessary. I shifted uneasily in my swivel-chair and thanked her. There was a faint pink on Stella's cheeks as she went in back to our minuscule washroom to put the first-aid kit away.

'You want to tell me about it again?' she said when she returned.

I shook my head, instantly regretted it.

'Not until after I've had coffee,' I said.

Stella's smile lasted her all the way to the glassed-in alcove where we do the brewing-up. Today she wore a pale blue silk dress held in at the waist with a thin gold belt with a metal buckle. The brave vibration as she walked was certainly taking me this morning. I had a job to concentrate on the sunshine outside the window after her image had disappeared behind the ground-glass screen.

'What did Prosser say?' she called.

'He wasn't too happy,' I said. 'Not about the case. That was the curious thing. He was more concerned with my injuries.'

'That shows a proper spirit,' Stella said. 'And proves the man has a heart of gold.'

'He's got a purse of gold too,' I said. 'Otherwise the whole thing would be a dead loss.'

'You mustn't become mercenary, Mike,' Stella said soothingly. 'We're not in this for the money.'

'There is that,' I admitted. 'It's just as well because I'd forgotten what the stuff looked like until yesterday.'

This time Stella's smile lasted her all the way back to my desk.

'We'll have you as right as rain in a few minutes.'

She sat down opposite in the client's chair, looking at me with very blue eyes.

'You figure the girl was the one? The one who came to Prosser's yard to make inquiries about Brown?'

'I wouldn't know,' I said. 'Prosser seemed certain. But I guess we're on the right track. That blonde number hadn't gone up there to play pinochle. The hard man was laying it into her when I showed up.'

'She didn't seem very grateful, Mike,' Stella

said critically.

'She tried to help by beaning the opposition,' I pointed out.

Stella shrugged well-sculptured shoulders beneath the blue silk dress.

'She almost brained you too. That may have been deliberate.'

'It hadn't escaped me, honey,' I said. 'She might not have been keen to speak to either of us.'

Stella got up to go back to the alcove. I closed my eyes against the gold oblong of sunlight that showed at the window. The little iron men with hammers had stopped beating on my skull now but there were faint echoes from time to time if I moved around too quickly. You'd best book yourself in to the local old people's home if this goes on, I told myself.

Association of ideas, I guessed. I'd passed a big poster for Sunset Homes real estate development on my way in. Apparently striplings of under seventy weren't allowed in. The way I felt today I qualified in spades. The plastic-bladed fan went on pecking at the edges of the silence.

Stella came back, put the coffee down on my blotter, went across for her own and the biscuit tin. Then she sat opposite, keeping silent with that marvellous tact of hers, her eyes fixed on my face. I nuzzled into the brew, added a mite more sugar, feeling that I might live with a little care and kindness.

Stella cupped her hands over one smooth brown knee and rocked slowly to and fro, still keeping her eyes on mine. I rattled my spoon rather unnecessarily loudly on the rim of my cup and selected one of my favourite butter-nut fudge specials from the tin.

'I'm waiting,' Stella said.

'I'm an invalid,' I said. 'I have to be given special treatment today.'

The smile at the corners of Stella's mouth flowered by another two millimetres.

'You get special treatment every day,' she said.

I thought we might be getting on dangerous ground so I changed the subject. The bulk of the Smith-Wesson .38 in its nylon harness made an insistent pressure against my chest muscles as I turned in the chair. That's what I should have been wearing yesterday. Things might have been very different then. Or on the other hand they might not.

I stared again at the big man's piece which lay on the edge of the blotter. Like I figured the registration details had been filed off. Labs have ways of bringing up such figures but I didn't want to ask official help. To do that I would have to tell the whole story to the police. I wasn't ready for that yet.

'You want me to ring?' Stella said.

My face must have registered something baffling. I was halfway through another gulp of

70

coffee and Stella gave a little exasperated snort.

'That number you brought back, goof.'

I put my coffee cup down on the saucer with rather more force than I had intended.

'If you think it will do any good. Like I said, I thought it was probably rented accommodation.'

Stella was talking about the phone number of the bungalow. I'd taken a note of it before I left the previous afternoon. It might have come in useful. And that way we had a method of tracing the real owners. If necessary. Because I didn't want to have to stand the racket of the damage up there. It would have been covered by insurance in any event.

Stella frowned at the sheet of paper in front of her and pulled my phone across. She sat still for five minutes after she'd dialled, her head bent, the sun butter-yellow on her hair, listening to the dialling tone.

'Nobody there,' she said at last.

'Like I figured,' I told her.

Stella put the phone in the cradle and pushed it back toward me. I finished off my cup, my thoughts a million miles away, my physical pains receding until they were only a faint memory.

'I'm still waiting,' Stella said patiently.

I ran through the salient points again, watching her gold pencil racing across the paper as I went on sipping my coffee. When I

71

finished she tapped with the pencil on very white teeth.

'You'd like my observations, I take it?'

I grinned.

'Over lunch. I'm taking you out today.'

Stella raised elegant eyebrows.

'That's news to me,' she told the filing cabinet.

'It has been known,' I said. 'And while we're briefly in funds . . .'

'You needn't go on,' Stella interrupted.

She riffled through her notes while I finished off the coffee. When I looked up it had gone quiet. She was absorbed in something on an inside page of the *Examiner*.

'We got it all wrong, Mike,' she said at last.

She pushed the paper over toward me.

'They identified your Mr Brown who may or may not have been killed out at Cocos Island.'

'I don't follow you,' I said.

Stella shrugged, her eyes fixed on my face.

'He was in the same business as us. He wasn't a mobster at all.'

'You'll have to spell it out,' I said.

Stella gave one of her elegant little snorts.

'Figure it out for yourself. It's all in the paper. He was a private detective.'

2

When I came down from the ceiling Stella had gone back to her own desk. The savage pecking of her typewriter sounded like she was attacking the keyboard. I stared across at her before turning to the *Examiner*. She'd ringed the down-page item in red ink; later she'd clip it for our files.

I read it through with mounting incredulity. Not that the facts were way out. But simply because I'd based my suppositions on the premise that Brown was a phoney. The name that belonged to the corpse fished out the bay was Reardon. That didn't help me any. He was a private operative all right. He worked on the other side the L.A. basin and he was pretty good according to his record.

The *Examiner* staffer had only written a few sticks of copy but it was densely reasoned stuff and there was a lot of information in the few paragraphs. The article didn't say what Reardon had been working on when he'd been hit. But he had six bullet holes in him, any one of which would have been fatal. It was heavy stuff; .45.

I stared over at the pistol on my desk. That was .45 calibre. I opened it up. It still held three unused shells. I unloaded the weapon and put it and the used and unused shells in my desk drawer and locked it, giving the key to Stella. I don't like loaded guns around. Leastways, those with hair triggers that are lying on desks.

The Smith-Wesson was a different matter. That only goes off when I want it to. Guns with hair triggers are in a class by themselves. I'd been careless with that. But then I'd been a little agitated by the events preceding the departure of the hard man and the blonde girl. Stella stopped attacking her typewriter and looked across at me.

'Where do we go from here, Mike?'

'Lunch,' I said, looking at my wrist-watch.

She didn't take the hint.

'It's only twelve-thirty. And I was talking about the case.'

'I'll think about it,' I promised her. 'Right now I'm concentrating on Reardon.'

Stella put her head on one side, the gold bell of her hair shimmering under the lamps.

'It turns the case around, doesn't it, Mike?'

'A little,' I admitted. 'But there's a lot of useful information in this article. And I didn't have to invest in a deal of leg-work to get it.'

'You think that pistol took Reardon out?'

'It's possible. But we shan't know until we can get it matched up with ballistics.'

'Which means the official force,' Stella said.

I nodded, leaning back in the swivel-chair.

'Time enough when we get the character who fired it.'

Stella smiled faintly.

'You won't find him by polishing your pants with your seat cushion.'

I grinned.

'Don't you mean the other way around?'

Stella shook her head.

'Not from where I'm sitting. Have you seen the seat of your pants lately?'

'I didn't bring my circus contortionist's kit with me,' I said.

Stella studied the cracks in the ceiling with dangerous languor.

'When you take them off at night,' she said. 'They're so finely polished you could shave in them.'

She put her head on one side.

'Come to think of it maybe you did just that this morning. You seem to have missed one side of your face.'

I matched her stare.

'I'm an invalid, remember. That side of my face was too painful.'

'You poor thing,' Stella said.

'This dialogue must now cease,' I said. 'I want to read this cutting again.'

Stella glanced at her own watch.

'Then we go to lunch,' she said decisively.

'And after lunch?' I said.

Stella runs the office so I figured I ought to find out what I was supposed to be doing next. She smiled again, like the same thought had occurred to her.

'Cocos Island?' Stella said. 'You should be thinking about it.'

I sat back in my chair and watched the smog and fumes rising from the stalled automobiles on the boulevard outside.

'It's too hot this afternoon. And too far for

today. But I'll think about it.'

CHAPTER EIGHT

1

It was already midday when I tooled the Buick off the main coastal highway and down the side lane to the section I wanted. It was a little cloudier today but the coolness was refreshing and there was a nice breeze coming off the sea. I checked again on the large-scale taped to the dashboard. I'd come some eighty miles farther up the coast because I could make the crossing in an hour that way.

While I drove I chewed over my conversation with Stella at lunch yesterday afternoon but the same old stale thoughts kept coming back. Now that Brown-Reardon was firmly established as a private operative the tentative house of cards I'd provisionally erected had come tumbling down pretty smartly. He could still be a crooked private detective, of course; we have a lot of those.

I wondered what his business had been out at Cocos. Stella had made discreet phone inquiries yesterday afternoon from a friend at Police H.Q. but she hadn't come up with anything startling. Reardon didn't run to a secretary; he was a one-man band who worked from his private home and it wasn't known what case he'd been working on—if any—

when he died. Which was helpful too.

The girl was the key here; I'd been really dumb over that one. I'd made a mental note of the registration number of her white sport job, but because of the traffic conditions on the way out to the house in the foothills had omitted to jot it down. I was paying for it now because after my knock on the head, the figures and letters had scattered to the four winds.

I hoped they would come back in time but they were hopelessly scrambled now; I knew they had something to do with an M and a U. That was as far as it went. Though I was certain it was an L.A. registration. Which was something. There couldn't have been more than three thousand white sport jobs with L.A. number plates.

I treated myself to a tight smile in the rear-mirror, my thoughts drifting back to the girl again. She'd been a looker all right. She obviously knew Reardon. Equally obviously she'd been working with him. Reardon could have been on the track of the hard man. Maybe he'd left some record with the girl. The phoney Brown disappeared and the girl was trying to trace him.

Then she turned up something which gave her the man whose pistol rested in my desk drawer. She went out to the house alone, which was a pretty stupid thing to do under the circumstances. If the hard man had already chilled Reardon. So he was slapping the girl around. But that didn't really fit. Because if he was Brown's killer he would probably have simply killed her as well.

Certainly the man who'd been trying to break into the *Glory B* had shot first time off, without hesitation. Prosser had remained alive by a miracle. Or had we got two killers? I couldn't get any answers to these questions until I caught up with either the girl or the hard man again. And I wouldn't be doing that in a hurry unless they came looking for me.

What I should have done was to have checked the girl's name and address from the details round the steering post of her heap. And those of the blue Mercedes as well. But I couldn't very well do that in front of the house in broad daylight without being spotted from the windows. It was difficult to avoid the feeling that I'd done my best but that my best on this occasion had been pretty feeble under the circumstances.

But Stella, as always, had helped to fill the gaps caused by my own deficiencies. She'd rung round the letting agencies yesterday after we'd returned from lunch. Like I figured the property up there was rented. I'd still had the wit to take a note of the name of the house and the boulevard before I came away. The real owners of the place were in Europe for a couple of months. And I figured the people who'd leased it wouldn't be coming back. Not after my dramatic entrance.

The opposition, whoever they were, must have been just as rattled by me as I was by them. I switched tracks again. Stella had also been working overtime last night. She'd checked out Cocos Island. It belonged to a well-known millionaire philanthropist called Martin Harrison. I didn't know a lot about him except that he was an art collector and eminently respectable.

It seemed unlikely that he would have been involved in Reardon's death, though the latter could have gone out to the island to see one of Harrison's employees, of course. I'd play it by ear, like always. Stella's thorough inquiries had established that Harrison was currently in residence. I could have phoned for an appointment but that would have meant tipping my hand.

In my book millionaires who own islands aren't usually very keen on seeing private eyes making inquiries about murder. Or even mayhem. So I'd decided to come on up anyway and trust to luck. Once I'd actually landed on the island I might be able to bluff my way through. And it was far more difficult to avoid seeing someone when they were actually in one's own backyard.

I'd got hold of Prosser again this morning before I left my rented house over on Park West and given him a guarded account of my activities over the past two days. He'd seemed incredibly grateful, though I actually hadn't done much to get his case any farther forward. If one could call it a case. But I'd warned him to watch out for anyone else who might be prowling about his yard. And told him not to go out there alone after dark.

He'd promised and I thought he'd keep it. Though he was a tough character all right he was just as vulnerable to bullets as the next man. I hadn't taken him entirely into my confidence, of course. The fewer people who knew the exact score the better. Not that I knew the score myself. But I had an idea the thing was going to get rougher as it went on.

I was certain now the Reardon kill; the girl; the hard man; and the attempt on Prosser's life were all connected. I didn't know how or why; it was just a hunch. But I make my living by hunches and survive the same way. I almost caught myself smiling as I drifted the Buick on down the dusty beach road and pulled up in front of a big sign which said: SEA-GOING VESSELS FOR HIRE.

2

'What do you want out there?' Dad Corcoran said.

He was a wiry old man with sun-bleached white hair and an emaciated build but he was incredibly strong and energetic as I'd found when we'd shaken hands and later when he hauled me aboard his sturdy, sea-going fishing launch.

'Private business,' I said.

We'd been going about half an hour and the shore had receded to a faint blue line in the haze. Dad Corcoran twirled the wheel and spat expertly to windward.

'They're not very keen on visitors from what I hear,' he said.

I shrugged.

'I have an appointment, like I said.'

Dad Corcoran's eyes twinkled beneath his blue denim cap. He looked like Charley Grapewin in one of his more nautical roles as he stood braced in the wheelhouse. I sat on a cushioned bench opposite him, grateful for the breeze that was coming in through the open sliding windows.

'You're picking up the tab, Mr Faraday. But you don't look like a businessman to me.'

I grinned.

'Do you always do your best to put customers off?'

Dad Corcoran screwed up his eyes, staring out at the hard-etched outline of a sizeable island that was coming up the far horizon.

'Don't take offence, Mr Faraday. There's not much distraction in my job. I'm a student of human nature, you might say.'

'No offence taken,' I said. 'What do you know about the owner?'

The old man eased up on the wheel and

82

rested his right elbow on the edge of the starboard wheelhouse window.

'Mr Harrison? He's a millionaire, ain't he? He's got to be if he owns such a big chunk of Californian real-estate. But he ain't too keen on visitors from what I hear.'

I studied his face carefully. His eyes were screwed up now as strands of white hair whipped about his forehead.

'Standard routine for millionaires, isn't it?'

Dad Corcoran gave the wheel another twirl.

'Mebbe. Mebbe not. I hear stories. Funny things go on out there sometimes.'

I sat up on the bench.

'What sort of funny things?'

Dad Corcoran passed an oil-streaked hand across his mouth, fumbled in the pocket of his jeans for a crumpled pack of cigarettes. I offered him one of mine, shielding the match as I lit it for him. Then I lit one for myself. He was quiet for a moment or two, feathering out blue smoke which was chopped into segments by the sea-breeze. I leaned back, watching Cocos Island becoming clearer and sharper through the big wheelhouse window, the bulk of the Smith-Wesson making an insistent pressure against my chest muscles.

'Crazy parties. People throwing one another off jetties. Even had a visitor drowned once.'

I screwed up my eyes against the brilliance of the sun which was now beginning to burn through the haze.

'Seems standard for millionaires' parties.'

Dad Corcoran hunched his shoulders, shifting gear on his cigarette until he had it in the corner of his mouth.

'I wouldn't know about that, Mr Faraday. I never mixed in such circles.'

He grinned suddenly, giving his face a certain rakish charm.

'Perhaps that's why I've lived a lot longer than some of those characters. Sensible life style.'

'You can say that again,' I said.

I glanced at the black silhouette of the island. It was becoming sharper and clearer by the minute.

'What else do you hear about Cocos?'

The old man whistled tunelessly through his teeth, altering course so that we were bucking through a cross-current, bow to wind.

'There's a certain amount of security there. Guards, dogs; that sort of thing. But then I guess you could say that's standard too.'

I thought about it for a moment.

'Is there a way you could get me ashore there without being too public?'

Dad Corcoran grinned. The wrinkles round the corners of his eyes looked like a relief map now.

'So you got no business there.'

I shook my head.

'I have business there. But not official.'

Dad Corcoran's smile seemed to bisect his

entire face.

'Why didn't you say so before, Mr Faraday? This is more like it. I'm your man for anything out of the ordinary.'

He passed the back of his hand across his mouth again.

'There's two public jetties on the south here. If you're going incognito you won't want those. There's a little bay on the north, that runs in between rather tricky rocks. That's the reason it's never used.'

'But you know it?' I said.

Dad Corcoran eased the launch farther out to leave Cocos amidships.

'I know everything around this section of coast, Mr Faraday.'

'You think you can get in all right?'

Dad Corcoran spat again, looking reflectively at the blue-green wavelets that splashed alongside.

'I can get in all right. It's like a mill pond today. How long would you want ashore?'

'Can you give me a couple of hours?' I said.

He nodded.

'No problem with the tides hereabouts. I can guarantee you a couple hours. But I'll have to stand off for that time. I'm too old to go courting trouble.'

My grin matched his own.

'Two hours will be long enough,' I said.

85

CHAPTER NINE

1

We got ashore in a tiny notch of a bay fronted by rocky cliffs that rose about a hundred feet from the shore-line. Dad Corcoran was good. I had to give him that. With engines idled back he drifted with the current through a maze of jagged rocks that just broke the surface. I left it all to him but I could see by the expression of his eyes, and the tightening of his fingers on the throttle controls that he knew exactly what he was doing at all times.

He was a real pro and as I was a pro myself I enjoyed seeing another at work in his own metier. Though I didn't tell him that, of course. He grunted as the keel grated into soft sand.

'You might get your heels wet but that's the best I can do,' he said.

'It's great,' I said. 'But you're cheating. You've been here before.'

He flipped his cigarette butt over the side into the clear water that ran over the sandy bottom, his eyes fixed up over the edge of the cliff.

'If you get caught you don't know me from nobody.'

'Your English is funny,' I said. 'But I get the

message.'

'What if you don't come back in two hours?' he said. 'It's something dangerous or you wouldn't be carrying that pistol.'

'I didn't know it showed,' I said.

Corcoran grinned.

'It doesn't,' he said. 'But I deliberately brushed against you when I hauled you aboard. I felt it then. I like to know who I'm carrying. Like I said you're no businessman.'

I looked him straight in the eye.

'You're wrong there,' I said. 'I'm here on business. Private eye business. I figure I'll be all right out here. But if I don't come back in the time allowed ring up Lieutenant McGiver at L.A. Police H.Q. and tell him what you know. The number's in the book.'

'I can read,' Dad Corcoran said.

He rooted in among his flying white hair with a long, oil-encrusted fingernail.

'Trouble is I don't know anything,' he complained.

I walked up to the bow and shook hands with him.

'You know enough,' I said. 'I've gone to see Harrison. And I guess you remember the geographical location of Cocos, don't you. So that even an L.A. flatfoot and his squad can find their way here.'

His smile seemed pasted on his face for a long time.

'I can remember that all right, Mr Faraday.

Anyone else you might want notified?'

'There's a girl called Stella,' I said.

Dad Corcoran's eyes had a faraway look.

'There's always a girl called Stella . . .' he said dreamily.

'Stop being a sentimental old fool,' I told him. 'She's my secretary. She's in the book too. I'll give you my business card seeing as we're partners.'

Corcoran took the pasteboard between a dirty thumb and forefinger and studied it like it might up and bite him.

'Sure, Mr Faraday,' he said mildly.

He cackled suddenly, like he'd just seen a secret joke.

'I'll see you later. If you're coming back.'

'I'm coming back all right,' I said. 'Just make sure you're here.'

'I'll be here,' he said in his absent voice. 'But if things get tough you might have to swim for it.'

'What does that mean?' I said.

He hunched up his shoulders again. He was getting pretty good at that.

'If there's any gun stuff I'll have to stand off a ways. I need to think of my health these days.'

I grinned.

'Sure. I understand that. I'll walk on the water if I have to leave in a hurry.'

Dad Corcoran hooded one eye in an elaborate wink.

'This ain't much like Galilee,' he said. 'Two hours, Mr Faraday.'

I was already jumping off the bow. I cleared the wavelets with a foot to spare. I went a ways up the short sandy beach, hearing the low throb of his motor as he went astern in the shallows. I got to a faint path which wound its way up between the boulders to the face of the cliff.

When I turned back the launch was already minute on the broad face of the sea; I couldn't even pick it out for a moment because it had a black hull and it was almost indistinguishable from the rocks between which it was threading its way. Dad Corcoran was certainly some helmsman. I saw a scrap of white flutter from the side window of the wheelhouse and I gave a wave in return.

I went up the zig-zag path scratched in the side of the cliff, trying to take it easy but within ten minutes I felt perspiration streaming off me. I was feeling pretty blown when I got to the top. There was a marvellous view from here but I had no time for the Fox Movietone travelogue stuff today. I couldn't see any sign of the launch now.

Then I realised Corcoran must have taken the vessel close inshore on the other side of the point. That way he would make it more difficult to spot from the land. I felt pretty lonely then as I turned and went up the last ten yards of path.

2

The island was about three miles long by a mile wide. It didn't seem much and it was just a speck on the map but it seemed a hell of a lot bigger on the ground. For one thing it was hilly in this section and I couldn't see across to the other coast when I got to the top of the cliff. And for another there was a mass of vegetation which masked the contours and made the place seem much more spacious than it was.

I decided to follow the rough path along the cliff-top and play it by ear after that. I knew Harrison had a big house out here; and even a helicopter pad. That was in the centre of the island. I intended to observe the place first and see what I could find out. But two hours didn't give me a lot of time.

It might have been better if I'd told Corcoran four but it was too late to think about that. I'd given myself half an hour each way to the house and an hour for a chat with Harrison. It was all beginning to sound impossibly cosy, like a brief walk in an L.A. park, now that I was actually here. Then I glanced at my watch and got a better sense of perspective; I'd only been ashore twelve minutes and already I'd come a fair way along the cliff-top path.

The sun and the breeze seemed temporarily

to ease my bruises though my ribs still ached from the double work-out with Lionel Prosser and the hard man up at the bungalow. I wondered whether he might be professional muscle employed by Harrison out here. It seemed unlikely but then a lot of unlikely things came true in Southern California. I walked on, coming to rolling country, the trees thinning until I could see across to the centre of the island.

There was a lot of shaved turf coming up with little flags; I couldn't make it out until I got closer but then I saw it was a full-scale golf course. There were even minute figures in sport-shirts and Bermuda shorts gathered on the greens. I went back under the cover of the trees then and regained the path. The character of the island was much gentler now and in another few minutes I came out on a bluff which faced inland.

There was a white mass in the far distance which looked something like a wedding cake. The big mansion made Hearst's San Simeon look like a garden shed and I could even see a yellow coloured banner floating from the top of the battlemented Gothic pile. Avalon, Mike, I told myself. You've finally gotten to Avalon.

But the world of fantasy didn't have Rolls Royce Silver Ghosts sprinkled about the driveway nor two swim-pools of Olympic proportions; one square which sat on a terrace out in front of the mansion; and another, the inevitable heart-shape around on the southern side. Both were full of blue-green water and swimmers and both looked pretty inviting because I was beginning to perspire heavily again.

I went down a shelving shoulder of hillside, keeping in the shadow of the trees, making sure there was no-one around. I worked my way in rear of the house where I could see operations more closely. It was obvious that Harrison was home and that these people were all long-term house guests. They wouldn't have brought their flash cars otherwise. But why they would want them for an island only three miles long was beyond me. Motor scooters would have done as well out here. Though, like someone once said, the ways of the rich are beyond understanding.

I stopped in the shadow of the trees and dabbed at my forehead with my handkerchief. I would have liked to have taken my jacket off but that would have made me too conspicuous up here. A man in a white shirt moving around against the heavy foliage. Or an off-white shirt would have been more correct. I gave myself a twisted grin and plugged on, conscious of the time again.

For some reason I had a sudden mental flash of the girl Diane Morris; the one who'd given me her address and phone number at the beach restaurant. She'd looked pretty nice. I might look her up again on my way back. She'd know a good deal about the movements of people in the beach area. The place was only a few hundred yards from Prosser's yard, after all. And she might even know the blonde girl I'd been chasing. Which would save a lot of time and work.

I should have been tired of Prosser's commission by now. I was no farther forward on the case, such as it was, than when I'd started. Though perhaps I was being unfair to myself. I'd only been working two days. And two major brawls in which firearms had been used wasn't a bad record. Even in my book. I plugged on down the hill, the image of Diane Morris growing fainter in my mind as I got closer to the house. I hoped Harrison had chosen something a little more original than Xanadu. It would be a distinct anti-climax when I arrived.

I hadn't got my story straight but with all his house-guests it was pretty obvious that if Harrison was mixed up in some funny business—and the murder of a private-eye was funny business all right—then he wouldn't be too keen to risk a straight confrontation with me in public. That was my insurance policy for getting off the island.

But if he were innocent that needed some thinking about. And I'd have to use a cautious approach. I was trespassing, of course. But an honest man who had nothing to fear wouldn't mind a mere gatecrasher who wanted to ask

93

him some legitimate questions. The difficulty was in framing the questions without raising suspicion in a guilty man and animosity in an innocent one.

You're becoming quite a philosopher, Mike, I told myself. I was telling myself a lot of things on Prosser's case. But then I spent a deal of time on my own when I wasn't getting my brains beaten out; and there was little else to do to kill the odd quarter-hour my kind of work threw up. And some of them were very odd.

I was in the shadow of a vast flowering hedge at the moment, only a couple of hundred yards from the sugar-cake house and the screaming men and women in the pool. I was maybe getting a little careless with the bird-song and the sunshine and the outdoor life.

Because I walked openly round the corner of the hedge and ran straight into a man with hard eyes and an ugly-looking shotgun. I was already in the air when he had it halfway to the firing position.

CHAPTER TEN

1

I saw the tall man's knuckles whiten as he flexed his fingers but my knee was already forcing the barrels upward as I slammed his jaw with my right. This case had been all rough and tumble so far and I aimed to be first off today. His eyes glazed and his fingers had already slipped from the triggers as I followed up with a hard left.

He went sprawling back across the turf and ended up against the trunk of a pine-tree, pinned there for brief seconds before he slid down slowly. I caught the shotgun barrels as the stock hit the ground and lifted it quickly, in case the safety catch was off. There was no explosion so I guessed it was a different sort of set-up this afternoon. The cards were coming right off the top of the deck.

I was in back of the hedge and had the Smith-Wesson barrel up against the side of the tall man's head before the flickering of his eyelids showed that he was coming around. I waited a few seconds more until he was fully conscious.

'You can have it the hard way or the easy way,' I said. 'Which is it to be?'

He made a gagging noise and bit his lip

before he had proper control of himself. He had some difficulty in clearing his throat.

'The easy way, mister.'

'That's better,' I said. 'So don't call out.'

I stepped back, broke the shotgun and ejected the cartridges before stowing it beneath the hedge. I'd already run my hands over the guard's pockets while he was out. He was clean all right.

'It's too nice a day to get punctured,' I said. 'So just do as I say.'

The tall man's muddy brown eyes stared into mine.

'You won't get very far, mister.'

'I don't want to get very far,' I told him. 'I just want a short interview with your boss.'

His jaw dropped slightly.

'Mr Harrison?'

'If the island belongs to him,' I said.

He nodded slowly, passing an unsteady hand across his jaw. I knew how he felt.

'Just point him out,' I said. 'I'll do the rest.'

His eyes flickered uneasily.

'You don't wish him any harm? It would be more than my job's worth.'

'It will be more than your life's worth unless you play ball,' I said. 'I don't wish Harrison any harm. Just a little talk, that's all.'

He gave me a long, puzzled look, started to get up. I stepped back, still keeping the Smith-Wesson on him.

'How do I know I can trust you?'

96

'It cuts both ways,' I said. 'Besides, you attacked me first.'

The tall man shrugged. The smouldering look had gone from his eyes now, to be replaced by professional resignation.

'It looks like I ain't got much choice.'

'You're a pragmatist,' I said.

'Whatever that is,' the tall man said.

He was up now. He was tall all right and broad with it.

'You give me your word you're on the square about Mr Harrison?'

'For what it's worth,' I said. 'I give you my word.'

The big man's eyes were still fixed on mine.

'He's a good employer, Mr Harrison,' he said softly. 'I wouldn't want anything to happen to him.'

'Nothing will,' I said. 'Unless he dies of old age while you're still shooting off your mouth out here.'

The guard shrugged impatiently.

'I just wanted to make sure. I can't afford to make mistakes in my business.'

'You just made one,' I said. 'And you have no choice.'

The tall man let out a long, low sigh.

'Guess you're right, mister,' he said. 'I got a jeep on the gravel path in back here. It'll be quicker that way.'

I checked my watch. Half an hour had gone by exactly since I quit the beach. I was well up to schedule.

2

The house, when we got up to it, was only slightly less pretentious than Versailles. I guessed it had been built in the high flush of the twenties when people could afford that sort of thing. Come to think of it some people could afford that sort of thing today. Certainly Harrison, judging by the ostentatious wealth on display here.

The guard drew the jeep up in rear of a group of tennis courts which were shaded by flowering hedges and tall palms which made an avenue either side. He had calmed down when we were driving up toward the house and as I was sitting behind him I'd put the Smith-Wesson away. It only made me look conspicuous among all these P.G. Wodehouse trimmings.

But now he looked resentful again as he set the brake of the jeep and killed the motor. He fiddled around with the sleeve of his left wrist.

'You broke my wrist-watch strap when you slammed me up against that tree,' he complained.

I grinned. I got out the jeep, keeping behind him as he sat in the driving seat. I reached for my wallet, fished out a ten dollar bill. I stuffed it down in the pocket of the tall man's windcheater.

'Go buy yourself a new suspender belt,' I told him.

He scowled but he kept the money. I was surprised by my own generosity. Then I figured the tab was coming out of Prosser's pocket after all. And maybe this guy was only an ordinary security guard employed to patrol Harrison's grounds. He was merely doing his duty and I had roughed him up a little.

I stared across to the tennis courts. There was nobody on them but I could see the girls in the terrace pool from here. Some of them were topless and there was some pretty interesting scenery on view. I turned back to the man at the wheel.

'Are you going to fetch Harrison or do I have to dive in and find him myself?'

The guard got out the jeep pretty quickly.

'Don't do anything hasty, mister,' he mumbled. 'If you find yourself a seat under the umbrella there I'll try and locate the boss and ask him to come out.'

'Be discreet,' I said. 'We don't want any more trouble.'

The guard nodded and went away, walking very fast on the balls of his feet. I guess his professional pride had been injured. I wandered up to the far end of the terrace, back from the pool area, taking obscure gravel paths that bisected the lawns, keeping to places where I wasn't likely to run into any of the guests.

Though it was against my inclination. Some of the guests had very pretty contours. The female ones, that is. It was too hot for all that stuff. It was almost as humid underneath one of the blue umbrellas when I sat down in the white-painted wrought-iron armchair that would probably have cost me a month's salary. If one could call it a salary.

I had no sooner got there than a young man with slick black hair and a white uniform with gold braid epaulettes materialised from somewhere behind. For a moment I thought I'd wandered into one of the swankier L.A. hotels.

'What is your pleasure, sir?' he said in a high, uptight voice.

I could have mentioned a number of things but I figured my kind of cracks wouldn't go down too well out here. I was waiting for Edward VII to show up on the terrace but he seemed to be holding fire for the moment. So I just ordered an iced lager and sat back to enjoy a few quiet moments of the assignment. I hadn't had too many so far.

Though Stella would have considered it pretty tame for me. About Force 2 on the Faraday Scale. I hadn't come across one corpse yet. Though there was still time. Especially if the hard-faced man at the bungalow showed again. He might even be on the staff out here for all I knew.

So I kept my eyes peeled though I was doing

my best to look like one of the idle rich. And the pressure of the Smith-Wesson was constantly nudging me back to alertness as I shifted my butt on the seat of the metal chair which was heating up nicely now.

The sun had burnt off all the haze and was coming in strong under the edge of the umbrella so that I had to screw up my eyes against the glare. It was then I saw something pink move out from the white bulk of the wedding cake house and come down the steps to the main terrace with long, easy strides. The guard I'd outed was hurrying in rear with an obsequious air so I guessed that the slim man in the pink shirt and white duck trousers was the owner of all these goodies.

He passed the people splashing in the pool as though they didn't exist, seeming to move on castors to avoid a sudden splash of water over the tiling of the surround as he glided by. I got up from the table and waited for him to come to me.

CHAPTER ELEVEN

1

As he got closer I could see that he was a lot older than I'd figured. He had silver-grey hair cut en brosse and a mustache of the same shade nestled in the deep grooves at the sides of his mouth. His pink silk shirt was buttoned at the throat and a matching pink silk tie was knotted in beneath the collar tabs. With the white duck trousers he favoured straw-coloured canvas sneakers like he was just going out to his yacht and a very expensive gold oyster watch glinted dully at his left wrist.

The man in the white jacket came up at the run then with my lager and the two met about twenty feet away from me. The houseman's eyes flickered anxiously at his employer but the smile at the corners of the latter's mouth merely broadened.

'An excellent idea. I would like one of those also, Carlos.'

The pair were almost up to me now and the wary brown eyes were inspecting me closely.

'Be my guest,' I said.

The smile widened and the slim man in the pink shirt held up his hand with a deprecating gesture.

'I am the host. Please avail yourself of the

facilities. I'm afraid I didn't catch your name or gather what you are doing here.'

He dropped easily into a metal chair opposite and waved me down too. I took my first sip at the lager, watching the figure of the man Carlos in the white regimental jacket. He was actually running now.

'Faraday,' I said. 'Mike Faraday. Shall I start now or wait until after Carlos gets back?'

His smile widened.

'Let us wait by all means,' he said equably. 'I have all the time in the world. I am sorry the atmosphere of money offends you. But I can assure you the attitude of my employees is entirely of their own making. It is not something I insist upon.'

I took another sip of the lager, saying nothing. It was great on a day like this.

'You, I take it, are a free man,' Harrison said at last.

I took him to be Harrison, of course, though he hadn't bothered to introduce himself.

'Hardly,' I said. 'But as free as one can be until the money runs out. Then I have to start back in the saltmines again.'

He nodded casually, still studying my face. He had an amiable, easy manner like many men of wealth and power and I was beginning to feel badly thrown off course. To use Dad Corcoran's nautical terms. Harrison wasn't at all what I expected and I began to figure I might have made a mistake in coming out here.

Harrison folded his well-manicured hands on the table in front of him.

'You are a private detective, are you not, Mr Faraday?'

'I didn't know it showed that much,' I said.

He smiled again.

'They are a somewhat piratical breed. I must admit I admire the type. I have something of that in my own make-up.'

'We should get on just fine, then,' I said.

He gave me another look at his white, even teeth.

'Let us hope so. Ah, refreshment!'

Carlos was back now, wheeling a tall metal trolley on rubber wheels, his face a mask of perspiration. He plugged a length of flex into a metal socket set in the low stone wall surrounding a flower bed in back of us. As the flex ran to the trolley the man in the white uniform wheeled carefully in between us I gathered it was a portable refrigerator cabinet. Like I said the rich are different.

'Just in case you wanted a refill, sir,' Carlos said deferentially to his employer, keeping his eyes turned down as he poured Harrison's lager into a crystal goblet which bore the latter's incised initials. Carlos didn't exactly genuflect but I thought he might any minute.

'I'm sure Mr Faraday would like another,' Harrison said cheerfully.

104

He took a sip at his glass with a satisfied expression. Carlos hovered anxiously until dismissed with a casual wave of the silver-haired man's hand.

'How did you get out here, Mr Faraday?' Harrison said, putting his glass down on the white metal surface of the table. Like everything' else about him the movement was neat, tidy and economical. I guessed that was maybe the way the rich got rich.

'By boat,' I said. 'A hired launch. It was important or I wouldn't have trespassed upon your time or property.'

'So I should hope,' he said mildly, but his eyes had grown hard and bleak.

It's something I've often noticed with big businessmen. They're like those chocolates with soft centres. Except with them the process is reversed. Smooth, creamy chocolate outside. Inside, the hardest of hard centres. You're getting pretty handy with the similes today, Mike, I told myself.

'You roughed up my guard, Mr Faraday,' he said evenly. 'That's something I don't like.'

'I didn't like it myself,' I said. 'He was coming at me with a shotgun.'

Harrison looked at me steadily, his slim fingers folded round the stem of his goblet.

'That is his job, Mr Faraday.'

I nodded.

'Sure, Mr Harrison. And it's my job to avoid holes getting drilled in me. Don't you think it's

105

an excessive reaction, even in defence of private property?'

Harrison looked down at his nails carefully.

'I don't think I know what you mean, Mr Faraday.'

I decided to give him a couple of barrels of my own.

'I think you do,' I told him. 'I'm talking about murder. That's why I'm here.'

2

'Murder?'

There was genuine shock in his eyes now. Even bewilderment. The conviction I'd had since I met him was growing. The noise the bathers in the pool were making seemed to be blotted out. They'd faded into a dim, indistinguishable babble. Harrison tightened the grip of his fingers round the crystal until I saw the goblet tremble.

Then he took another long sip, screwing up his eyes against the sun, which was beginning to penetrate beneath the shade.

'I think you're going to have to explain yourself more fully.'

'I intend to,' I said. 'And I'd like some answers before I leave here.'

He shrugged, still holding the goblet halfway to his mouth. His eyes were fixed on the distant line of hills, beyond which lay the sea. I took a quick glance at my watch. I still had more than an hour before Corcoran was due back. Things were fine.

'I don't see how you expect me to help you, Mr Faraday,' the man in the pink shirt said. 'We don't go in for murder here.'

He smiled thinly.

'Maybe,' I said. 'But I have a client who delivered a Mr Brown out here about a fortnight ago. He was disembarked at your own private jetty. That was the last time he was seen alive. His body was washed up near Bridport Inlet. But I guess you know the place. It's a ways down from Palos Verdes.'

'Really?'

There was nothing but polite interest in Harrison's voice now. He took a slim, gold cigarette case from the pocket of his trousers and selected a cigarette. He proffered the case to me but they were a kind I didn't use and I thanked him politely. He lit up, using a slim gold lighter that broke away from the edge of the case.

It was that sort of set-up. And he was that sort of a guy. He looked at me shrewdly as he feathered out blue smoke.

'Just what are you implying, Mr Faraday?'

'Nothing,' I said. 'I'm just looking for information. Brown was last seen alive out here on Cocos. The island belongs to you. So I come to see the owner. It's as simple as that.'

Harrison gave me a look of grudging admiration.

'As you say, Mr Faraday, fair enough. I think I know you, don't I? I read something about you in the *Examiner* last year.'

'They print a lot of rubbish about me in the *Examiner* from time to time. I shouldn't believe all you hear.'

He smiled again.

'I don't, Mr Faraday. I own a chain of newspapers in Canada, among other things.'

'Bully for you,' I said. 'But Canadian newspapers aren't really in the top league. To rate big in that field you want New York, Paris and London.'

He opened his eyes a little wider.

'So, you are a connoisseur of the international newspaper scene now? Thank you for the advice.'

I grinned.

'It was sincerely intended. And I do know what I'm talking about.'

'I'm sure you do,' he said blandly. 'But we were talking about murder, were we not?'

'It's a fascinating topic,' I said. 'And if you can give me any help I'd be obliged. Brown was a private operative, too, incidentally. His real name was Reardon. Mean anything?'

Harrison shook his head slowly, his eyes fixed intently on my face.

'I give you my unqualified word that I've never heard the name nor seen the gentleman in question. But perhaps my word's not enough for you?'

I shook my head.

'I'm happy to take it. I'm a pretty good judge of human nature. And why would a man like you lie over a thing like that?'

He nodded approvingly, the sunlight catching the gold watch at his wrist.

'Why indeed? I like you, Mr Faraday. You are a man who makes up his mind in a hurry. I could use someone like you in my organisation.'

'I'm sure,' I said politely. 'But don't tempt me. Not this afternoon, with the sun-dazzle on the pool and all these gorgeous girls around. I might compromise my principles.'

Harrison leaned forward and gave a long, low laugh.

'The answer I expected. But I felt I ought to try. So you want my help. You think your Mr Brown or whatever his name was might have had business with one of my employees out here?'

'You catch on quick,' I said. 'It's possible.'

Harrison took another sip of his lager, reached in the top of the freezer cabinet with a muffled apology, and broke out another bottle for me, opening the cap with a gadget on the edge of the refrigeration unit. He poured it expertly for me, his eyes studying me closely.

'It's possible,' he agreed.

'How many employees do you have on the island?' I said.

He wrinkled up his forehead.

'Between thirty and forty. Including the outdoor staff and the people who run the boats. There is an easy way to find out what you want.'

He held up his hand and Carlos came down at the run, this time carrying an ivory telephone on a long flex. He plugged it into a socket protected from the weather by a metal shutter in the same section of wall as that supplying the freezer.

'Excuse me a moment.'

He spoke in clipped tones.

'Is Mr Holt on the island? Good. Please ask him to come to the terrace as soon as possible. It's a matter of some importance. Thank you.'

He put the phone back in the cradle and crossed the long legs in the white duck trousers.

'Gary Holt is my estate manager out here, Mr Faraday. He will know or can certainly find out what Brown was doing here and whether he left the island or not.'

'He was met by a big man with an Alsatian dog,' I said. 'My informant returned some while later and was told Brown would be taken back to the mainland in one of your own vessels.'

Harrison nodded curtly, the sun glistening on his silvered hair so that it looked burnished in the strong light.

'That is useful, Mr Faraday. That would be Dad Corcoran, I suppose? He's quite a

110

character around these parts.'

I shook my head.

'My client came from a ways down the coast. It took some hours to get here. That's another of the things I'd like more information about.'

'You and me both,' Harrison said.

He looked up as a shadow fell across the flagstones.

'Ah, here's Holt now. Perhaps he will have the answers to some of your questions.'

CHAPTER TWELVE

1

The man who came forward to join us wore an immaculate blue blazer with silver buttons and the same sort of white drill trousers affected by his employer. He had black patent-leather hair and a clipped Ronald Colman mustache. He had a clipped British voice to go with it and I put him down as an ex-Army officer who'd landed in California.

In the thirties he'd have done a David Niven and gone over big in movies but in today's Hollywood climate with most of the major studios closed and the real action moved over to Europe he'd have done exactly what he had in this instance. Latched himself on to a nice easy job with a tame millionaire. He smiled faintly like he guessed what I was thinking and dropped casually into a chair opposite.

'You wanted me, M.H. ?'

'That's right, Gary. We have a little problem here. I want it tackled with discretion.'

He smiled at me apologetically.

'Forgive me, Mr Faraday. I forgot to introduce you. Mr Faraday was inquiring about a visitor we had a fortnight ago. A Mr Brown. Apparently he landed at the main jetty and was met by one of our guards. The launch owner who ran him out was told on his return that our own staff would take him back to the mainland.'

Holt wrinkled up his forehead in concentration. He reached out across the table and gave me a hard, dry hand to shake.

'Glad to meet you, Mr Faraday,' he said pleasantly. 'I didn't get your status in this matter.'

'I didn't give it,' I said.

Harrison smiled briefly, turning to the other man.

'We want this tackled with discretion, Gary. Tact is the word. I'll explain later. Right now all I want is for you to run a check among the outdoor staff. Find out what Brown's business was; who he came to see; and who ran him back and at what date and time.'

'Will do, M.H.' Holt said in a crisp, official voice.

I glanced at my watch again.

'I have just an hour,' I said. 'There's a launch coming back for me then.'

Holt waved his hand airily, reaching out to the freezer chest at Harrison's extended permission. He rooted around, came up with a bottle of orange juice and a straw.

'No need to worry,' he said casually. 'It won't take me more than twenty minutes.'

Harrison's smile widened at my expression. It was my reaction to the orange juice, of course.

'Holt's a hard drinker,' he explained.

The estate manager smiled too, showing a wide expanse of white teeth. He must have been quite a charmer with the ladies.

'I make it a rule never to drink before six o'clock, Mr Faraday. It's quite a temptation on an estate like this.'

'I can imagine.'

Holt shot a quick glance at his employer, gauging his possible reaction.

'I can't afford to behave like the guests.'

Harrison had an equable expression on his face. He sipped delicately at his iced lager, shielding his face from the sun with the back of his hand. The man in the white uniform was still hovering in the background.

'There is a difference in status,' he said blandly. 'Had you not better check out Mr Faraday's queries? Just in case it takes longer than twenty minutes?'

There was a slight edge to his voice now and I caught a glimpse of the power that the millionaire normally kept reined in. Holt got up quickly, scenting danger. Small red patches were burning on his cheeks. He gave me a little half-bow.

'Be back in a quarter of an hour, Mr Faraday,' he mumbled. 'Like I said, this shouldn't take long.'

He went off, walking stiffly on the balls of his feet. Harrison looked after him absently.

'A good man, Holt,' he said softly. 'But he

114

occasionally forgets himself.'

I said nothing, just went on sipping at my beer. Harrison glanced at me approvingly.

'You have tact, Mr Faraday. I like that quality in a man.'

I shrugged.

'I know enough to keep my mouth shut, Mr Harrison. You're calling the shots here.'

Harrison tapped with thin fingers on the edge of his goblet, making a high tinkling sound.

'That is something my staff are sometimes inclined to overlook,' he said.

He looked across at the man in the white jacket.

'Of course, if you had more time, I'd offer you a late lunch . . .'

'You're very kind,' I said. 'But not today, unfortunately.'

Harrison made an expressive movement of his shoulders.

'A pleasure deferred. In the meantime feel as free to enjoy yourself as any of the other guests.'

'This is fine,' I said. 'I'll just enjoy the scenery.'

2

Holt was true to his word. He was back within fifteen minutes. He wasn't exactly running but from the length of his stride and his determined air I gathered that Harrison's gentle admonition had had the desired effect. There was a rime of perspiration on his well-bred gentility as well as on his forehead as he dropped himself into the chair he'd vacated a short time before.

'You were right, Mr Faraday,' he said, ignoring his employer, who sat with his hands clasped together on the warm table surface.

'Mr Brown did come out here.'

He consulted a small blue notebook he produced from his blazer pocket. He rattled out a date and time which tallied with what Prosser had told me. I took a note myself on the back of an envelope I found in my billfold. Harrison watched us impassively as though the whole thing didn't concern him. It probably didn't, come to that.

I'd written him out of the case by then. He'd have to be the best actor in the world otherwise. There were so many people out here on Cocos, anyone could have knocked Brown off; out here or back on the mainland for that matter. Though I didn't let any of my doubts show on my face.

'I got hold of all the key people, Mr Harrison,' Holt said with an anxious glance at the millionaire. 'But I'm afraid I've no idea what Mr Brown wanted here or who he came to see. Is that important, Mr Faraday?'

'Pretty important,' I said. 'And I can imagine Mr Harrison would be concerned too.'

116

Harrison unfolded his hands.

'You bet your sweet life,' he said unexpectedly. He was addressing Holt and the latter made a spasmodic scribble in the blue notebook.

'I'll check it out in more detail, of course, Mr Harrison. But I've taken it as far as I can for the moment. I had to do the interviewing on the telephone, of course.'

'Of course,' I said. 'Mr Harrison knows where to reach me if you come up with anything else.'

I'd given Harrison one of my pasteboards while Holt was away and asked him not to spread my business around. Not that he was likely to. But I might want to come out to Cocos again and discretion was my middle name. Holt was still sifting through his notes.

'What else did you come up with?' I said.

The estate manager absently picked up the halfempty bottle of orangeade he'd left on the table. He sucked nosily at the straw.

'There I can help you, Mr Faraday. Mr Brown left the island pretty late. Around three a.m. He came down to the main boathouse where Albert was on duty. Albert himself took him over to the mainland in Number 2 guest launch. It's all in the logbook.'

He smiled apologetically.

'If you or Mr Harrison would like to see the books? Or can I get Albert up here.'

Harrison shook his head.

'I don't think it will be necessary,' I said. 'As long as Albert would be available if I ever want to come back.'

'Surely, Mr Faraday,' Holt said.

He was pouring on the charm now, for the millionaire's benefit.

'Have you any more detail?' I said.

Holt bent over his notes again.

'According to Albert the launch reached the mainland at 3.35 a.m. Mr Brown had a car parked in back of the beach, he said. He walked away from the jetty as Albert went astern with the launch. It was a fine, clear, moonlight night and he saw him walk down as far as the car-park. That was the last time, because he had to attend to the controls. When he got out about a quarter of a mile he saw the headlights of a car going away. That help at all?'

'Fine,' I said, though it added another pattern to the tangle.

I'd come to a complete dead-end here. Harrison got up quickly, coming forward to shake hands.

'Glad that's settled, Mr Faraday.'

There was relief in his eyes. Not that I blamed him. If I'd been in his shoes I wouldn't have wanted any scandal out at Cocos either.

'You can get in touch with me or Holt at any time. But let us know when you're coming. That will give us an opportunity to lay on lunch.'

'You're too good to me,' I said.

I watched him walk away in the brilliant sunshine toward the pool area. Holt stared after him too. It was difficult to read his expression because he was sideways on to me.

'Mr Harrison can be very kind,' he said in a blank voice. 'And he can be other things also.'

I grinned.

'You're in a prejudiced position,' I said.

Holt turned toward me, a wry expression on his face.

'You can say that again, Mr Faraday. Like the man said, feel free to call on us at any time. How are you getting back?'

'By boat.'

Holt shook his head, not smiling.

'I meant to your boat.'

I glanced at my watch.

'Walk, I guess.'

Holt shook his head.

'Walk nothing in this heat! I'll run you back in the jeep. It will give us the chance to talk.'

I stared at him for a long moment.

'A gracious suggestion,' I said. 'I'll take you up on it.'

CHAPTER THIRTEEN

1

'Another dead end,' Stella said.

I shrugged.

'Not necessarily. Though we have only Albert's word that he took Brown back to the mainland.'

I frowned at the haze that was depositing particles of grit on the window that faced the boulevard. It was humid this morning and the smog that blurred the landscape outside seemed all of a piece with Prosser's case. If it could be called a case. Stella attacked her typewriter suddenly, the brittle pecking seeming to tear the silence apart.

'Give me notice next time you do that,' I said.

Stella glanced at me casually.

'My, your nerves must be in shreds,' she said.

I grinned, fingering the bruises on my face. They were a lot fainter today.

'What have you been doing in my absence?' I said.

Stella smoothed a stray hair into place on her immaculate coiffure with one pink-nailed finger.

'This and that,' she said casually.

Rather too casually I thought.

'Which means you came up with something,' I said.

Stella attacked her typewriter again.

'You mustn't read too much into my impromptu remark, Mike. And even I'm not infallible.'

'You surprise me,' I said.

Stella gave me a long stare from very blue eyes.

'You do want some coffee this morning?'

'I'll be good from now on,' I promised.

The phone buzzed while Stella was brewing up. I got to it first. It was a girl's voice, low, well-modulated.

'Mr Faraday?'

'In person,' I said.

There was a brief silence at the other end of the wire.

'Who is that?' I went on.

'You wouldn't know me, Mr Faraday. But I owe you a good deal. You can call me Kathy.'

'That's nice,' I said. 'What can I do for you?'

'I'm in a good deal of trouble and not moving around very much,' the girl said. 'Can you come over to me? As soon as possible.'

'You want to talk a little more first?' I said.

The girl's voice was hesitant now.

'Not really, Mr Faraday. I'd prefer to speak to you in person. It's terribly urgent.'

'All right,' I said. 'How did you get on to me?'

'Through the book, Mr Faraday. You know the Alcazar Apartments?'

'I'll find it all right,' I said.

Stella was at her own phone now and took down the location.

'It's Apartment 1111,' the girl said. 'On the fifth floor. How soon can you make it?'

Stella was already checking from the large-scale we have pinned to the far wall. She held up one finger to me. I glanced at my watch.

'I'll be there around midday,' I promised her.

'Don't fail me, Mr Faraday.'

'I'll try not to,' I said.

There was a metallic click as she put the receiver down. I replaced mine in the cradle.

'She sounded pretty scared,' I said.

Stella nodded.

'You can say that again.'

She went over and fetched the coffee, re-seated herself in the client's chair. I rooted around in the biscuit tin for one of my favourite butternut-fudge specials, seated myself on the edge of the desk on the same side as Stella. That way I could look down at her. Which made a nice change.

'You don't really want to get involved in anything else,' Stella said.

I nodded. Like always she had a point.

'You have enough on your plate,' Stella went on.

'It may be something that can be cleared up

122

quickly,' I said.

'Let's hope so,' Stella said. 'You have a lot of high-powered brain work to do on Prosser's tangle.'

'I thought it was pretty open and shut,' I said.

Stella's unnerving blue stare threw me off. I got up from the desk and went back to my own chair, reached out for my steaming cup.

'Where were we?' I said.

'Just cracking Prosser's case, according to you,' Stella said.

'We still have that pistol,' I reminded her. 'We can have a check run on it in the police lab.'

'Not without a lot of explaining,' Stella said.

'There is that,' I conceded.

'And it still may not tell us anything,' Stella said.

I grimaced at the filing cabinet.

'Depress me some more,' I invited her.

Stella smiled happily. Today she wore a striped outfit that seemed to have been sprayed on, which was shooting my morale to hell and back. But it looked just right on her. Stella had impeccable taste and she always knew what to wear. Or what suited me, which was more to the point. But it needed a lot of self control on hot days like now. Stella's smile widened.

'Kathy,' she said in a dreamy voice. 'She sounded nice.'

'She'll probably turn out to be an old lady who tips the scales at twenty stone,' I said.

Stella went on smiling.

'That's your standard line, Mike. I've seen some of your old ladies at the other end of phones. They usually come up as twenty-year-old nymphomaniacs with fantastic figures.'

'I should be so lucky,' I said modestly.

Stella looked at me mockingly.

'We'll see,' she said mysteriously. 'Shouldn't you be hitting the road for the Alcazar?'

By the inflexion of her voice she made it sound as far away as Spain. I glanced at my watch.

'I just have time for another cup,' I said.

I was still remembering the dancing rhythm of Stella's magnificent curvature when I rode down in the creaky elevator to street level.

2

The Alcazar Apartments, when I got to find them, were an impressive block that seemed to have been carved from one piece of marble and fitted with chrome insertions as an afterthought. They were set back among acres of barbered lawns where the sprinklers were going, amid bronze fountains, bougainvillea and all sorts of other frippery. It was a pretty nice set-up. And it would have been a pretty nice rental.

I found a shady corner beneath a grove of

palms and killed the Buick's motor. I went on over pink tarmac, my size nines slapping echoes from the façade of the building, inhaling the smog which tasted great today, watching the twelve-storey block float up the sky and conscious of the lonely thumping of my heart. It had a double echo today, no doubt due to the rebound from the bulk of the Smith-Wesson in the nylon holster.

I hoped there wouldn't be a receptionist and a phone system when I got in the lobby because I didn't know the girl's surname and it would look pretty funny asking merely for Kathy.

But there was no-one around in the big marble concourse with its tessellated pavement and I buttoned my way up to the fifth floor in a teak elevator cage that had been so waxed and burnished that I could see my reflection in the opposite wall. It was so distorted I thought my injuries had come back, though Stella had assured me that the bruises had mostly died out today.

I went on down a corridor floored in a white carpet whose pile caught me beneath the knees and hit the brass bell-push set in the doorpost of 1111. There was no reply for a moment and then I heard the faint vibration of a girl's heels on parquet beyond. The door was opened without hesitation though I knew I'd been quizzed through a spyhole set in the door.

The girl who opened it was really something. She was pretty tall, a shade under six feet and her figure went in and out in all the right places. Her shimmering blonde hair was worn shoulder-length and was held in place by a white bandeau. She had a pleasant open face with smooth, tanned features; very white teeth beneath broad, sensual lips and wide green eyes. She was around twenty-eight years old and was enjoying every minute of it. I liked her.

'Mr Faraday?'

There was a flush on her cheeks now and a hesitancy in the voice but it was the same one I'd heard on the phone.

'Sure,' I said. 'You did say around noon and it's just a minute off now.'

The flush deepened and she opened the door wider.

'Please come in. You must forgive my slight agitation. I'm in some difficulty.'

'That's all right,' I said.

I followed her in to the hall of the apartment and waited while she locked and chained the door behind us. The precautions had seemed a bit elaborate to me all the way up here because I'd noticed the closed-circuit TV cameras along the corridors and I knew my approach to the apartment had been noted and videoed from some control room in the block.

The girl wore a pale blue sweat-shirt and

brown linen trousers that moulded her figure closely. There were no rings on her fingers and the clear varnish on her nails reflected the light as she put up her hand to her hair.

'Through here, Mr Faraday. I thought we'd have a drink on the balcony.'

'Sounds great,' I said.

She led me through a vast living room where light sparkled and reflected on furniture and pictures, striking down through parchment blinds at the big windows. Beyond the sliding French doors there was a cool-looking terrace floored in pink tiles with cane furniture scattered about and lots of greenery growing in artificial beds raised up and held by walls of rough stone.

There were also enormous ceramic pots set about the terrace in which flowering bushes were set and the air was filled with the perfume of tropical flowers. There was a metal trolley with an assortment of healing waters at one side of the circular metal table and I was reminded of yesterday, albeit on a slightly more reduced scale.

'Would white wine be all right, as it's so close to lunch-time?' the girl said. 'There's plenty of ice.'

'Fine,' I said.

I dropped into one of the cane chairs, watched her closely while she did cool-sounding things with long glasses and ice-cubes. I couldn't quite place her but it would come to me.

'You have a surname I take it?'

The girl moved uneasily, her back to me.

'I'll get to it, Mr Faraday,' she said defensively. 'I could do with a drink and I'm sure you could too. It's very close today.'

I kept on staring at her back as she went on pouring the wine. It was one of the nicest backs I'd seen all week.

'You didn't ask me here to chat about the weather,' I said.

The girl made a little clicking sound through her teeth. Whether she was irritated by my questions or had spilt some of the wine I couldn't make out. It wasn't important either way. I turned my attention from her to the wall of green that fringed the balcony and cast a welcome shade in here.

'No, Mr Faraday,' the girl said, bringing the glasses over.

'But I am in trouble and I'd like to conduct this interview in my own way and my own time.'

'Sure,' I said. 'I understand. And I appreciate the hospitality.'

The girl gave a fleeting little smile then, which transformed her face. She leaned forward to chink her goblet against mine and then sat down opposite with a swift, liquid movement.

'You said something about owing me a debt.'

128

I took a first sip at the wine. It was the best. I started inching the contents of the glass down my throat. It seemed to ease all the dust and stickiness of the day away.

'I don't get it.'

The girl put her glass down carefully near the edge of the table. She shook the blonde hair that tumbled about her shoulders.

'You have a short memory, Mr Faraday,' she said calmly. 'Though I must admit I was dressed and made up a little differently the last time we met.'

I stared at her without saying anything. She was taking a long time coming to the point. But then most numbers like her did. Especially when they were in trouble.

'My name's Kathy Green,' she said, her eyes fixed on my face. 'Leastways, that's my professional name. I'm a journalist and specialist writer. My real name's Kathy Reardon. John Reardon was my brother. You saved my life when Nikko tried to kill me out at the bungalow the other night.'

CHAPTER FOURTEEN

1

I let out my breath. The girl's nervous smile lingered as she continued to study my face.

'You must figure I'm a pretty smart operative,' I said. 'Not recognising you as soon as I arrived at the doorway.'

Kathy Reardon shook her head.

'Like I said, I'd changed my appearance. I didn't want to be seen in my own persona that night. And I'm terribly grateful to you.'

I grinned.

'How grateful?'

The girl stood up and came round the table quickly. She bent and kissed me fiercely on the mouth. The kiss seemed to go on for a long time and when the roaring in my ears had cleared the girl took her mouth away and held my face in her two hands.

'That and a good deal more, Mr Faraday.'

'Call me Mike,' I said. 'Now that we're friends. But I'll settle for another glass of wine pro tem.'

The girl smiled a smile from which all strain and tension had gone. She went back over to the trolley. Her vibrant movements reminded me of Stella. I could start a stud-book with all the form that was on display today.

'How did you trace me?' I said. 'You didn't know me from Adam when I came through that window.'

'I was in shock,' the girl said. 'You didn't bother to announce yourself.'

'There wasn't time,' I said.

I took the glass from her. She sat down in the cane chair next me, her cool fingers resting on the back of my hand.

'I had a good reason for lighting out, Mike. My life was in danger but I waited until I knew you were safe. Nikko took off like he was on a space-mission.'

'I was passing out around then,' I said. 'But I had noticed.'

'I drove out and parked a ways down the road,' the girl went on. 'I waited a couple of minutes but you didn't show. I wanted to follow you, see where you lived and find out who you were before thanking you. And also discover what on earth you'd been doing there in the first place. You see, I was afraid Nikko might come back.'

'We'll get to all that,' I said.

'I went down the row of parked cars, copying the licence details,' Kathy Reardon said. 'When I got back here I checked out the phone book. Yours was the only name that fitted. There were no other private eyes in the lineup.'

'You should have been a P.I. yourself,' I said.

Kathy Reardon shook her head grimly, the

corners of her mouth turned down.

'My brother was in the same business as you, Mike,' she said evenly. 'It didn't do him any good.'

I was silent for a moment.

'I'm sorry about that,' I said. 'I'm working on the case already. I knew he'd gone out to Cocos Island. I was there yesterday.'

The girl gave a little startled cry and her fingers tightened on my hand.

'It seems we have a lot to talk about, Mike.'

'True enough,' I said.

Kathy Reardon got up and re-filled her own glass. For the first time her sleeve went back and I noticed once again the gold bangle on her right wrist.

'Why did you want to trace me?' I said.

The girl shrugged.

'I should have thought it was obvious. Firstly, because I wanted to thank you, most sincerely, for intervening when you did. Secondly, I thought we might pool our resources. And thirdly, when I found out who you were, I felt you might carry the fight on on behalf of my brother.'

'I'm already doing that,' I said. 'So part of your plans coincide with mine. Who was that character with the pistol? And what was he doing out at that bungalow?'

The girl's eyes were shadowy with fear.

'His name's Nikko, like I said. I think he killed my brother.'

'But what was he doing there?' I said.

The girl put slim fingers round her goblet and leaned forward, lowering her voice, like we could be overheard in the secret greenery of this secluded roof-garden.

'My bet is he was searching for something. Maybe notes on the case my brother left behind.'

'But why would your brother have left stuff there?'

The girl's mouth curled at the corners in a little quizzical expression.

'Sorry, Mike. I'm telling it badly. John was renting the house for a few weeks from a couple who were away. It's my guess he was frightened for his life. That's why he left his own place in L.A. and he wasn't around the usual spots any more.'

I looked at her for a long moment. Kathy Reardon smiled and leaned over to pour me my third goblet of wine.

'I guess we'd better start right from the beginning,' I said.

2

I'd completely forgotten the faint roar of the traffic now. The rooftop garden was so dense with foliage and vegetation on the street side that the smoke from my cigarette went up in an almost mathematically straight line toward the sky, when it was suddenly dispersed as it left the shelter of the greenery.

'It all began some months ago,' Kathy Reardon said. 'My brother hinted he was on to something big. A large syndicate organising jewel robberies in the East. Shipments of diamonds mostly. The stuff was flown out to the West coast to be disposed of. The large stones cut up or re-mounted; the rest sold through jewellers and converted into laundered money.'

I nodded, watching a big commercial airliner high up, starting to turn to take its place in the stack for descent to L.A. International.

'So that's it,' I said. 'Standard procedure. They're back into diamonds now. Drugs and diamonds give the best returns. Precious stones are safer; they're easy to deal with because they take up so little space; and they don't have to be smuggled in. So the mobs merely have to organise a chain for disposal within the States, without crossing international borders. Easier all round.'

The girl's green eyes were still fixed on my face like she was hanging on my every word. I was beginning to like her more by the minute.

'That's what my brother said. He had an obsession about a Mr Big out here in Southern California.'

I gave Kathy Reardon one of my best lazy smiles.

'He had a wide choice,' I said. 'There's

134

dozens, ranging from crooked politicians with organisations in Washington to local crime kings. He surely didn't expect to smash a diamond syndicate on his own? Who was he working for?'

The girl shook her head.

'He wouldn't say. He hinted he had government backing. That Federal agents had to work within the law and that he wasn't bound by such restrictions.'

'Sounds like an old recording of me,' I said. 'I take your point. But it all begins to make sense of the case I'm on. It's obviously the same set of circumstances in which your brother was involved. And with the focus on Cocos Island. He was getting close. Too close. So he had to be taken out.'

The girl shivered, showing the strain now. Her eyes held the haunted, uneasy look I'd seen before.

'There's a man who owns Cocos Island, Mike.' she said. 'He's a millionaire.'

'I know,' I told her. 'I went out there to see him yesterday. I asked him specifically about your brother. He was extremely co-operative. For what it's worth I don't think he had anything to do with your brother's death.'

The girl's eyes were wide with amazement.

'You took a chance. Going out there in broad daylight?'

'I'm used to taking chances. I set myself up, if that's what you mean. But I more or less eliminated Harrison, the man who owns Cocos. Organising diamond thefts would be peanuts for an operator of legitimate enterprises on his scale. He deals in hundreds of millions, and he seemed as anxious to clear up the matter as I was.'

The girl stared at me without saying anything. The breeze was making a faint rustling sound in the undergrowth behind her now.

'But I took a raincheck on Cocos itself,' I said. 'Harrison employs a lot of people out there. Any one of them could have been mixed up in something. And one or more of them could have hit your brother. The estate manager mentioned a character who helps to run the launches. He says he delivered your brother back to the mainland and that the last he saw of him was when he was walking away.'

The girl bit her lip.

'That's more than I've been able to find out, Mike. And it could be true. Maybe the island had nothing to do with his death. He could have been killed after he got back.'

'By Nikko?' I said. 'You haven't told me about him.'

The girl's face changed, her features seeming to physically darken.

'I'm coming to that, Mike. Speaking of John's car, it never did turn up.'

'Maybe the people who took him out dumped it somewhere,' I said. 'It could take

136

months to find. The L.A. Police haven't come across it according to the press reports.'

The girl nodded.

'So you called at Prosser's yard inquiring about Mr Brown,' I said. 'And Prosser gave you all the information he had.'

'I guess Mr Prosser told you that.'

'Sure,' I said. 'He's my client. Only don't spread it around. He was worried about Brown. He thought he might have been up to no good. Then you making inquiries had him puzzled. What bugged him most, though, was that someone tried to kill him aboard his boat the *Glory B* a few evenings after. The same craft he took your brother out to the island on.'

The girl's face had turned chalky white now.

'That could have been Nikko, the man you tangled with the other day.'

'That's what I want to hear about,' I said. 'How come you got tied up with him.'

The girl shivered, putting her fingers round the stem of her goblet. She waited for the rumble of the aircraft circling overhead to die away a little before she replied.

'Like I said, Mike, there's a lot of money involved in the racket John was investigating. The last time I saw him he mentioned Nikko. He was a professional strong-arm man mixed up with the mob who were organising and carrying out the jewel raids in the East. My brother was worried in case they turned their

137

attention to me. All I can think of is that John might have had some information they wanted. Or else he'd found out too much.'

I lit another cigarette.

'What sort of information?'

The girl shook her long blonde hair.

'That's what I don't know, Mike. My brother showed me a picture of Nikko he'd got from police files. I forget the man's real name. He was of Eastern European extraction, I think.'

'What were you doing down at the boatyard the other afternoon when Prosser spotted you?' I said. 'He pointed you out and I followed.'

'I wanted to have another chat with him,' Kathy Reardon said. 'My brother had told me he was hiring a boat from Prosser Marine to go out to Cocos. That was the reason I went to see Prosser the first time, of course. Before I knew John was dead. I hung around a long time but you were always talking together. It looked like being a heavy wait so I decided to try again another afternoon.'

'Instead you went back to the bungalow,' I said. 'Why?'

The girl took another sip at her wine.

'I'd visited John there a number of times. He'd given me a key. I thought I'd try to find out if he'd left anything for me. A note or something like that. It was the first time I'd been up there alone and without meeting him by appointment. I was surprised to see that car outside but I thought it might have been the police.'

'So you walked right in?' I said.

The girl bit her lip.

'It was stupid, looking back on it. But the front door was wide open. I couldn't see any harm. The big man was there. I recognised him as Nikko from John's photograph. He was just starting to search the room.'

'He must have been pretty sure of himself to leave the front door like that.'

The girl shrugged.

'He was. It's an isolated place and he wasn't expecting anyone. But he must have heard my car drive up so he obviously saw me through the window. I think he would have killed me if you hadn't turned up.'

'What did he tell you?' I said.

'He ordered me to hand over the letter or paper my brother had given me. He'd beat it out of me or worse. My going there was proof I knew something.'

The girl's eyes were dark and troubled now and her voice broke.

'If it hadn't been for you, Mike . . .'

I wasn't listening now. It was the rustling in the foliage that interested me. It had been troubling me for some minutes. There wasn't that much of a breeze, even at this height.

I saw the sunlight glint on dark metal. I threw myself across the table, hurled the girl backward. We both went down in a tangle of cane furniture and broken glass as the gun blammed twice and heavy slugs whined about the terrace.

CHAPTER FIFTEEN

1

The man with the butter-yellow hair and a thin face like a knife-blade was half-out the greenery when I got both hands beneath the big metal table. Kathy Reardon had rolled away somewhere on the tiling. I could hear her sobs of terror but I had no time.

The blued-steel automatic was halfway into the firing position when the table edge caught the hit-man under the chin. I heard a click like a bone had broken somewhere and he floundered over among the tropical flowers. I felt the sour taste of fear in my throat as I reached for the Smith-Wesson.

It was still in the nylon holster but I'd hit the tiling so hard that it had been jolted almost out the retaining clip. I had it now and I fired in the air. I couldn't see my man; he'd disappeared among the waving green fronds but I didn't want him drawing a bead on me from behind the screen of foliage. It had been a close thing and I'm not really allowed one mistake on serious cases, let alone two.

'Stay put,' I told the girl.

I was at the edge of the terrace now, in the shadow of a big tree that grew there. The earth behind the banked wall must have been about ten feet deep because the massive trunk gave me plenty of shelter. I didn't intend to leave it until I could see what I was aiming at.

Random impressions were flitting through my brain with the rapidity of images in an Eisenstein montage sequence. Fancy thinking, Mike, I told myself as I searched the greenery opposite for the faintest vibration of a leaf, my trigger-finger sweaty on the Smith-Wesson.

I gave a quick glance backward, mainly to see that Kathy had taken refuge against the face of the rough stone wall and was giving her well-known imitation of a limpet. I was interested in my own reactions this morning. I guessed the pistol merchant had climbed up the outside fire escape to the terrace.

Whether he had intended to hit me or the girl was an interesting question. I realised he might be lying unconscious beyond the shrubbery a few yards from me but I'd be going blind at the wall of green and the trigger-man wouldn't miss a second time. This wasn't the day for suicide; the sky was too blue and the sunlight too brilliant. Don't try it, Mike, I told myself.

The time to have gone in there was a fraction after the metal table had hit him under the chin. But I hadn't been ready then and there was no time now to think about it. I heard a faint rustling noise and the tip of a bush to my right centre was moving in a way no bush ever moved in nature. I guessed then that my man was lying half-conscious or maybe fully conscious against its base, where the impact of the table had thrown him. He was moving away. I figured he wouldn't hang around now that his attempt had failed.

The crack of the shots might have been muffled by passing aircraft and some people may have mistaken them for backfires but he wouldn't risk being caught in the open in broad daylight like this. It must have been pretty important to have brought him up here. And he wouldn't hang around for the police to show. I decided to wait a minute or two more and try and get him on the fire-escape.

I quit the tree then and wriggled down the terrace to join the girl. She was trembling, her face white and she turned wide eyes to me as I put my arm round her shoulder and drew her close.

'You all right?'

She nodded.

'Don't worry about me. I'll just stay put.'

We were talking in low voices but I was still facing frontwards and I wouldn't miss a move if the hit-man tried anything else. I wondered if he'd heard all our conversation. If he had he might have figured he'd gained all the information he needed and had then tried to silence the girl. That was interesting too. I'd sift through our dialogue later.

'Where's the fire escape?' I asked.

'Way over to the right.'

'Is there any way he can get back into your

143

apartment from there?'

Kathy Reardon shook her head.

'There's a big brick buttress comes out near the French windows, which helps support the terrace and the roof garden. He'd have to come back down this end again to get inside.'

'That's all right, then,' I said.

I saw some fronds of ornamental bamboo move slightly. They were rippling from left to right. I knew where I was now.

'I'll be back in a minute,' I said.

'Take care,' the girl whispered.

'I'll sure as hell do that,' I said.

I got over the rough stone wall on to dry earth, wriggled in among the tropical ferns. I felt like Errol Flynn in Objective Burma. Except that we weren't using blanks. After about thirty seconds of cautious gut-work I came out in a drainage runnel next the main wall of the roof-garden that must sit atop the face of the building.

It was half overgrown with plants but there was enough light left for me to see down the far end. Something dark was moving painfully up the metal ladder that led to the sky-line. It was difficult from where I was lying but I got off a snap-shot, half-deafening myself with the detonation in the confined space in here.

2

There was a lot of powder-smoke and my ears

were singing but I felt better as I saw the half-glimpsed figure jink erratically before disappearing. I got up quickly and ran down the runnel, brushing through the leaves and small branches that whipped at my face. The Smith-Wesson holds five so I still had three in the chambers. Ample now that I'd have the advantage.

I pounded on down, careless of the noise I was making. Maybe it was a mistake. I was thinking sloppily again. I should have waited a little until I could hear the man with yellow hair on the metal treads of the fire-escape. He might even have had somebody with him. As it was I got up the short metal ladder and looked down over the parapet.

The hit-man's slug took out a half brick about a foot from my head and blinded me with dust. I darted back quickly, stung by my lack of professionalism. But my reflexes were working fine now. The tall man was standing on the fire-escape landing one storey down, half hidden by the treads. My third shot hit the metal platform a yard from where he was standing, striking vivid red sparks from the metal.

Yellow-hair went over backward like he'd been poleaxed and I heard the clatter of his feet on the treads of the next flight. I turned back then. I'd made my point. I'd be a sitting target if I followed him down; especially if he waited on the ground. People were already gathering in small knots in the street. I went back through the shrubbery on to the terrace like Paavo Nurmi in his heyday.

I told the girl to ring the law and to stay inside. I ran through her apartment and rode the express elevator down to the ground floor. Fortunately there was no-one waiting on my level but even so it seemed like a hell of a long time. I put the Smith-Wesson back in my holster as I burned up marble over the concourse.

I went round the side of the building into the alley, the crowds, the traffic and the noise of L.A. a faint blur both to eye and ear. I'd maybe taken forty seconds to get here but it felt like a lifetime. There was a mass of people in the alley entrance and I had to force my way through.

The man with the yellow hair was just on the last section of the escape when I got up close in the shelter of parked automobiles. He got off another slug when he was halfway down and the crowd scattered. The second shot from his automatic must have hit the gas tank of the car whose shelter I'd just quitted because it went up in a sheet of yellow flame.

There were screams and cries from the people in the alley now. The heat was so fierce I felt my hair singeing and I moved quickly away, the wavering figure of the gunman long and insubstantial in the heat-haze that was hovering over the burning scarlet sedan. I

146

didn't hear the explosion; it was a curious aural effect but the next thing I remembered was being blown along the ground, cartons and old beer cans whirling in a crazy chaos about me. I could taste blood in my mouth but I was facing the right way and I could still see the yellow-haired man beneath the suspension of the nearest parked car.

He was firing in the direction of the crowd. I pumped off my last two shells very carefully, supporting the wrist of my gun-arm with my left. Yellow-hair suddenly broke the even rhythm of his stride and went into an eccentric dance. When he ran out of steps he found he was dead. I didn't need to examine him for that. I'd seen the same thing too often. And I'm a pretty good shot.

But I took time out to re-load the Smith-Wesson from the spare clip I always carry in the holster. I felt properly dressed again. I got up feeling old and tired and beat-up. It was only then that I was conscious of the roaring sound the burning automobile was making and the screaming noises from the crowd. I walked slowly over to the crumpled figure of the yellow-haired man, keeping the Smith-Wesson on him all the way just in case the age of miracles hadn't passed.

The automatic lay a foot from his stiffening fingers and I kicked it farther off. I didn't pick it up because that would have ruined it for prints. The hit-man was dead all right, the front of his jacket a crumpled mass of scarlet. I avoided his accusing eyes and bent to find his billfold, trying to avoid staining my fingers. I got it out in the end, found his driver's licence.

According to that and some letters in another compartment, his name was Albert Modena, living at an address on Cocos Island. I treated myself to a wry smile. I couldn't prove it right off but the odds were that this was the character who'd brought Kathy Reardon's brother back from the island. If his form was anything to go by, either as dead meat or, if not, in that same condition soon after.

I put the stuff in the big guy's pocket and went over to the entrance of the alley, the crowd falling back. A middle-aged man was lying on the ground and there was a white-robed nun bandaging his leg. That was the only casualty as far as I could make out.

'It's all right, sister,' I said. 'Don't be afraid.'

She looked at me with clear, mild eyes from behind gold pince-nez.

'I'm not afraid, sir. You seem to be on the side of the angels today.'

I grinned.

'Something like that.'

I told her who I was and where I could be found when the police arrived. Then I went back around the end of the apartment block, walking fast, my breath hammering in my throat. As I did so a black sedan that had been parked farther down went away very fast, making a screaming noise with its tyres. It was too far off for me to read the number-plate so I couldn't have done anything about it in any case.

But it was obviously the back-up car for yellow-hair. I figured my thoughts earlier had been in the right direction. I went in through the main entrance and found I was still holding the Smith-Wesson. I put it back in the holster and rode up to Kathy Reardon's apartment. The girl had put the table and chairs upright and was sitting slumped in one of the latter, drinking another glass of wine.

Her face was still white but she seemed to have recovered a little as I sat down opposite her. She poured me another slug. I looked at my watch then. Incredibly, it was only a quarter after one. I was beginning to feel hungry.

'I saw everything that happened, Mike. It was horrible.'

I nodded.

'The guy who came up here was called Albert Modena. He lived on Cocos. It's a cinch he was the one who killed your brother. According to the estate manager, Holt, he was supposed to have taken him back in the launch to the mainland. Either he was dead before he left the island or dropped off on the way over.'

The girl stared at me for along moment.

'But you evened the score, Mike. That's

something else I have to thank you for.'

'We'd better get our stories straight,' I said. 'The police will be up here soon. What was that character after? He wanted to knock off one of us. Or both. Did he come for information? Or had he heard what he came for and decided one of us was expendable?'

Kathy Reardon gave a comic little shrug, her face numb beneath her tousled blonde hair. Suddenly, unexpectedly, she smiled. She was physically bracing herself as she stood up briskly, like an actress preparing for a part.

'Your guess is as good as mine, Mike. It's something we'll have to talk about this afternoon. How about lunch?'

I lifted my eyes to the cool tranquillity of the terrace. On the next block of apartments I could see a row of curious heads, blurred by distance. From below the ragged roar of the crowd still came up, now overlaid by the first of the prowl-car sirens. 'Sounds great,' I said.

I switched my gaze on to the drinks-trolley. 'We'd better get some bourbon out here right away. The boys in blue will need a little sweetening up.'

CHAPTER SIXTEEN

1

Stella's eyes were serious as she stared at me and the girl across the desk surface. I'd filled her in on the diamond angle and Modena and she'd spent an hour taking notes. It was late afternoon now and shadows were lengthening through the plastic blinds that softened the smog and the stalled traffic on the boulevard outside. Kathy Reardon gave a nervous little cough. The colour had come back into her cheeks but my eyes hadn't left the rear mirror all the way across town.

It would have been a tough session with the cops except that an old friend, Lieutenant McGiver of Homicide had been one of the first plainclothes men on the scene. We'd worked together from way back and I'd filled him in on all the points I thought he needed to know. Like Stella said the rest of the stuff was mere supposition for the moment. Besides, it was all too complicated. The Reardon kill was being handled by the police up around Palos Verdes and we didn't want to involve them at this stage.

I'd asked McGiver to go easy with the press announcements so far as Kathy Reardon was concerned and we'd lit out before any pressmen showed. It had been difficult to get away, not because of McGiver's suspicions but because even the uniform boys had made the Reardon number's terrace their temporary headquarters and the liberal supply of booze and other refreshments hadn't given them any inclination to move.

McGiver had initially given the case a different slant by labelling the Modena kill a fire-escape shoot-out, which avoided him making Kathy's address public. My bringing her here not only got the press off her neck but removed all further danger from whoever had sent Modena. Someone else was in back of it, of course. Most likely the diamond heist syndicate if what the girl's brother had told her was true. He had always played straight with her, she'd told me.

'I wondered if you could find Kathy a bed for a day or two,' I asked Stella. 'She'll have to lie low for a bit.'

The two women looked at one another approvingly.

'You beat me to it,' Stella said drily.

I glanced at my watch. It was after five and I was still full of no coffee.

'You'd better go now,' I told Stella. 'Before the press catch up. McGiver has held back all the important facts in his releases till now but he can't hold off much longer.'

'Right,' Stella said briskly.

She turned at the door, fishing for car-keys

in her handbag.

'You sure you can survive without me for one evening?'

I grinned.

'It's been known,' I said.

The Reardon girl held out her hand hesitantly, like this was an extremely important social occasion.

'I can't tell you how grateful I am, Mike.'

I shook my head.

'Let's wait until all this is over. And be careful.'

I turned to Stella.

'Ring me as soon as you get in.'

Stella shook the gold bell of her hair.

'You're stealing my words again.'

I still heard the creak of the elevator going down when the office was empty except for the faint slur of the traffic and the lonely beating of my own heart.

I didn't have long to be lonely. I'd only been sitting there about ten minutes before the phone rang. I couldn't place the voice. It was a man's, hard and impersonal.

'Mr Faraday?'

'The one and only,' I said.

'You're a difficult character to find,' the voice said. 'I been trying for some while to trace you.'

'We millionaires jet from place to place,' I said modestly. 'Do I know you?'

'We met briefly,' the voice went on. 'You

might say informally. I have a proposition for you.'

'I'm already busy,' I said.

'I think you'll find this worthwhile,' the voice said. 'It could be profitable. And it's about the case you're working on.'

I sat upright in my old swivel-chair, the deepening shadows etching the outline of the blinds on the carpet, not hearing the creeping surge of the traffic on the boulevard below.

'I'm always interested in profits,' I said. 'I don't often make any.'

There was a grudging sympathy in the voice now.

'You and me both.'

He paused.

'I'd like to suggest a meeting in about an hour's time. It's urgent.'

'I'll bet,' I said. 'Not too lonely a place. I'm in rather delicate health at the moment.'

There was another short pause on the wire.

'You name the venue if you're nervous,' the man said.

I shrugged, admiring the gesture in the window glass opposite, which gave back my battered face in a sardonic reflection.

'I'm not nervous. It's just that I don't know whether you're friend or enemy.'

There was a dry chuckle on the line.

'I'll take a raincheck on it. Rate me as friendly for the moment.'

'You got a name?' I said.

154

'Don't let's be formal,' the voice said. 'We'll go into all that when we meet. Like I said, you name the place.'

I thought for a moment.

'You know Bart's Bar? It's dark and discreet and fairly empty this early in the evening. And you will come alone?'

Again the dry chuckle.

'I'll come alone, Mr Faraday. And I know the joint.'

'That's fine, then,' I said. 'An hour, like you said. It'll be dusk then and discreet enough for both our purposes.'

'Sounds alluring,' the voice said. 'How will I know you?'

'I'll be wearing a rose up my right nostril,' I told him.

He was still thinking up his answer when I put the phone down.

2

Bart's was and is a square, dusty brick block with about as much character as an old bean can. From the outside, that is. Inside it was different; one entered by steep cellar steps and the long bar was got up like a thirties German beer hall with a lot of ancient posters for bygone Oktoberfests, varnished and in glass frames.

It was all right if you liked that sort of thing. I was indifferent this evening and I certainly didn't intend to lower quarts of the lethal German lager Bart brewed in his own set-up on the edge of L.A. I got there a quarter of an hour later than I'd stipulated, just to make sure my man was already inside. I didn't intend to let him get the drop on me in some dark booth while I was still trying to read the tab.

Bart himself was on duty tonight; he was a shy, self-effacing character of just under seven feet tall with a bullet head and a haircut to match that made Yul Brynner look positively hirsute. He gave me a bone-crushing grip that I felt all the way down to my socks.

'Hi, Mike. It's been a long time.'

'Too long,' I said.

I looked down the misty bar that seemed to curve away to infinity. There were only about half a dozen people in, like I figured there would be and I couldn't see a customer like I'd imagined my caller to be.

'Anyone looking for me?' I said. 'I'm supposed to meet a guy here. Big man, hard face, maybe with some damage.'

Bart gave me a gap-toothed grin. With his red and white stripe jersey that strained across his muscular chest and his shabby blue trousers he looked like a rejected take from Pabst's film of *The Threepenny Opera*. That was a joke too, because behind the bar there was an old framed poster for Pabst's Blue Label Beer. Association of ideas, maybe. You're in sparkling form tonight, Mike, I told

156

myself.

Bart nodded. Oblivious of all the trash that was rushing through my head.

'Guy came in about ten minutes ago. He fits your description.'

He grinned again.

'He had some plaster-work on his map. Looked like he might have been in a mild auto accident.'

'Maybe,' I said. 'Where did you put him?'

'I don't put them anywhere, Mike. Not unless they misbehave themselves. He went down in the far booth on the right under his own steam. It's called Munich.'

That was another of Bart's fancies. Each of his drinking booths was named after a German city. I looked around for A. Hitler in the encompassing gloom but he didn't seem to be in this evening.

Bart had his hand on the polished lever in front of him.

'What's your poison?'

'Something light and not potent,' I said, relishing the disappointment on his face. Bart took a lot of pride in his own brew. He came from German stock three generations back and like many people remote from their roots, it seemed to have reverted with him. He was crazy about anything to do with Germany between the wars; the Bauhaus, cabaret, Brecht and the kammerspiel particularly. My, we got culture too tonight, Mike, I told myself.

'Just give me a whisky with plenty of water and lots of ice,' I said.

'You're changing, Mike,' Bart said. 'Getting middle-aged and bourgeois.'

'Maybe,' I said. 'But I'm the customer. And the customer's always right.'

'Not in here,' Bart grunted.

He let go the lever and moved down the bar.

'I'll bring it over. There's no extra charge.'

I walked on down the aisle between the polished oak tables and the right-hand row of booths, noting the names of the German towns in their old-fashioned Gothic script. Each booth had paintings, prints and photographs of the appropriate city from various periods of its history. It was a pretty fancy idea and any other time I would have enjoyed it.

But not tonight. I had a fair idea of the man I'd come to see and I wasn't disappointed. He was seated in the Munich booth, his eyes narrowed to pin-points, watching me come down toward him, like a boxer watching his opponent coming into the ring. I felt a little like that myself. He had a piece of brown sticking plaster fixed between his eyes. That was where the girl had hit him with the poker.

When I had the corrugated iron face more clearly in focus I recognised him all right. He made Charles Bronson, Jack Palance and all those fellows look positively prissy. So I didn't intend to mess around with him. Like Bart had

158

told me his face showed other evidence of damage. He exhibited a wolfish smile as he gave my own face the onceover.

'It's like looking in a mirror,' he said in his hard voice.

'You have a point,' I conceded. 'It must be Nikko, as I live and breathe.'

The hard man shrugged his massive shoulders. Tonight he wore a thick houndstooth jacket and lightweight drill trousers. Dressed for all weathers. I decided to keep my jokes to myself. He didn't speak again until Bart had served my drink.

'So the girl told you,' he said.

I nodded, sitting opposite him, the bulk of the Smith-Wesson in its nylon holster pressing against my chest muscles.

'She told me,' I said.

His curious slate-grey eyes regarded me intently.

'I couldn't find her anywhere around after we met,' he complained.

'I'm not surprised,' I said. 'And you won't find her now. She's safely under wraps.'

He lowered heavy lids over his eyes, his big hands folded round one of Bart's vast steins of beer.

'Pity,' he said softly.

I shook my head.

'Leave her alone. She doesn't know anything.'

His eyes were alive with interest now.

'Which means you do?'

'Maybe,' I said guardedly.

He lifted the beer mug to his lips, wiped some foam off with the back of an impressively scarred hand.

'Looks like we have the makings of a trade.'

'Maybe,' I said again. 'What's your position in all this?'

'Hired hand,' he said.

'By the boys back East?' I said.

His eyes widened a fraction.

'Right. So my head's on the chopping block too, unless I come up with something fast. There's a lot of green stuff involved.'

'Like half a million dollars?'

I was making things up now but he bought it.

He shook his head slowly.

'You were misinformed there, brother. More than a million. I don't know the details. They never tell me much. It's my job to help get it back.'

'Who's the Mr Big?' I said.

Again the wolfish smile.

'Don't be childish, Mr Faraday. I only take my orders from the guy above me out here on the coast. I'm a freelance, at the other end of the phone in N.Y. You're a pro. You know how we work.'

'Sure,' I said. 'I know how you work.'

'So you might know where the stuff is,' Nikko said.

'I might,' I told him. 'If the price is right.'

His eyes were narrowed again, the voice very low and soft now.

'Oh, the price will be right, Mr Faraday.'

'What happened about the diamonds?' I said. 'You know that much?'

The curious eyes, like a snake's, flickered. They made me uneasy. If Nikko's hands hadn't been on the table all the time I wouldn't have sat there. But I didn't think he'd try anything in public. And I'd carefully checked out the few people in the place. A man like Nikko would work on his own. Like he said, he'd merely take his orders from someone higher up.

'What was Albert looking for?' I said.

The big man shrugged.

'The same thing. He was an amateur compared to me but he insisted on doing the job himself. I was told to take the wheel on this occasion.'

'So that was you going away from the alley pretty fast,' I said. 'Too far off for me to get the licence number. I thought it was the work of a pro.'

Nikko had a slightly self-satisfied expression on his face.

'It takes a pro to recognise one,' he said modestly. 'There isn't much job satisfaction any more.'

We might have been talking shop at a computer salesmen's congress. The big man

161

finished off the stein and looked up at the Gothic-style clock in the heavy wooden case screwed to the wall.

'Did you shoot at Alex Prosser on his boat at Bridport Inlet one night a few weeks ago?' I said.

The big man slowly shook his head.

'Not me,' he said softly. 'I never heard of the guy.'

I stared at him closely, believed him. He had no reason to lie and a character like him wouldn't care what I thought either way.

He glanced at the clock again.

'You'll have to meet my principal. He'll be very disappointed if I don't bring you.'

'But supposing I don't want to go?' I said.

A pained look passed across Nikko's face.

'Be reasonable, Mr Faraday. No-one's forcing you. But if it isn't me someone else will only come around. And my principal won't stop searching for the girl.'

I hesitated a moment, my thoughts whirling around without engaging the ratchets inside my skull.

'How did you find me?' I said.

The eyes were hooded now.

'Like I said, I'm just the hired help. I was given your name and asked to contact you.'

I inclined my head.

'Interesting,' I said.

Nikko agreed.

'What did you do with my Colt?' he said. 'It

162

was my favourite piece.'

'It's safe enough,' I told him.

Nikko cleared his throat.

'You'd do better to deal with a pro, Mr Faraday. Some of these people are amateurs but they got lots of power by just reaching out for a telephone.'

'You're right,' I said.

'Let's go meet your principal.'

I finished off the whisky, retained a melting ice-cube in the pouch of my cheek. I got up and went down the bar, settling the check for both of us. Professional courtesy.

Bart nodded curtly, his eyes holding a question as they raked over the big man at my elbow. My eyes followed his to the phone in the alcove. I shook my head almost imperceptibly. Bart gave me a tight-lipped grin.

Nikko was already going up the steps at the far end of the bierkeller. I followed him up and out into the purple dusk.

CHAPTER SEVENTEEN

1

'My heap or yours?' Nikko said.

'I'd prefer to drive myself,' I said. 'That way I'd feel I was coming back.'

The big man had deep shadows across his face in the neon-tinted dusk but it seemed to me he was smiling.

'We got a problem then.'

'Is it far?' I said.

He nodded.

'A ways,' he said vaguely.

'I could follow your heap,' I said.

His smile widened.

'It wouldn't do, Mr Faraday. It could look bad if you turned off somewhere and I didn't find you in the rear mirror. They might want my head.'

I grinned.

'Don't you trust me?'

'I'm a realist, Mr Faraday.'

'So am I,' I told him. 'We go in mine. You can pick yours up later. When we come back.'

Nikko shrugged.

'Have it your way.'

He fell in alongside me as we walked back to where I'd parked the Buick. I felt more relaxed now. I knew he wouldn't try anything until we got to where we were going. And I was more curious to see who his principal was than to bother about the outcome of the interview at this stage. Like always, I'd play it by ear.

The big man didn't speak again until he slid into the Buick's passenger seat.

'You carry a piece, Mr Faraday?'

'Of course,' I said. 'Don't you?'

It was difficult to make out his expression in the shadowy interior as I fired the ignition.

'Sure,' he said at last.

'That's all right then,' I said. 'I promise not to start anything if you don't. We have to trust one another.'

He nodded his head like I'd said something profound. There was a tinge of regret in his voice.

'That's just the problem, Mr Faraday. There's a fine edge to these things. And I like everything sewn up tight.'

I glanced at him as I tooled the Buick out into the traffic chaos of L.A. Slug-trails of green fire trailed up and down the canyons of the boulevards and the far hills were sprinkled with sequins where the lights of houses showed.

'There's one solution.' I said. 'If you don't trust yourself put your piece in the dashboard tray there. Then you have nothing to fear.'

Nikko nodded his head sagely, giving me his jackal smile.

'It's like politics,' he told the passing traffic.

165

'East and West stuff. No-one wanting to lay their arms down first. So we get to keep the status quo.'

I kept my eyes on the rear mirror. There was nothing suspicious but I was just making sure. Nikko hadn't given me any instructions when we hit the mainstem so I knew we were going in the correct direction.

'That's right.' I said.

He made no further comment except to give me a curt instruction whenever we got to a junction. It was about a forty-minute drive up into the foothills and the last streamers of gold and green and crimson were dying out the sky and staining the stippled surface of the Pacific as we got higher up.

The sea looked cold tonight; cold and inhospitable, the atmosphere emphasised by the remote speck of a sailing boat about three miles out, looking like a piece of fluff dropped on to that vast surface.

I turned my eyes back on to the road, registering automatically the big man's monotones as we took forks that led to ever increasingly lonely side roads. The place was well-chosen; a long, low bungalow that stood several hundred yards up a narrow lane, about half of that distance from the nearest house.

There was a U-shaped drive in front and lights punching out the squares of the porch-glass in the darkness. A beige saloon was standing in front of the porch and the Buick's headlight beams sliced across a For Sale board at the entrance to the plot.

'Another rented property?' I said.

Nikko shrugged.

'Not exactly.'

By his expression I figured he might just as easily have said that he'd broken in for a couple of nights. Or maybe just for this one interview. It was something I'd come across before in my line of work. I went all the way around the arc of the driveway and pulled the Buick up beyond the beige saloon. I was making sure of my retreat if I had to come out in a hurry. Nikko looked at my manoeuvre approvingly. He didn't say anything but I knew it was exactly what he would have done in the same circumstances.

He was already out the passenger door as I got down myself. I debated whether to leave the keys in the ignition but figured it was too risky. Instead, I put them in my right-hand trouser pocket where I could get at them in a hurry.

The Smith-Wesson felt heavy and reassuring against my chest muscles as we went across the gravel, rasping brittly in the darkness and the silence, to where the yellow squares of the porch windows awaited us.

2

Nikko walked alongside me instead of in rear

as most pros would have done. Despite his treatment of the girl he impressed me; not that I approved of his trade. He impressed me in the sense that he was open and outgoing in his dealings with me. He was a hired mercenary; cold and impersonal; and he'd been at some pains to make his position clear.

I knew he'd drop me without compunction if I got in his way; he'd proved that in our struggle out at the girl's place. But unlike many people I'd come across in my gritty career I knew instinctively he wouldn't let me have it between the shoulder blades without warning. He'd down me, sure as hell, if he possibly could; but he had certain rules about it, just as I had.

For example he was walking abreast of me at the moment, which put neither of us at an obvious disadvantage. Certainly, he had the slight edge; I was armed and he knew it just as I knew he carried a piece. But he could get at it and bring it to bear on me with his right hand; whereas my right would have to go left before coming back with the Smith-Wesson, which would make it an awkward shot.

He was behaving exactly as I would in the present state of armed truce. He smiled thinly in the porch light like he knew what I was thinking. I glanced at the heavy piece of sticking plaster that was almost equidistant between his eyes.

I'd seen the force with which Kathy had

168

delivered the blow with the poker and I marvelled at the toughness of his skull; I'd only caught the backlash and it had rendered me comatose for almost an hour.

I felt another twinge in my leg then as we got up the shallow flight of steps. The big man went ahead of me and opened the green-painted door, the surface of which was flaky and scaling. There was a distinct smell of mould as we got into the dimly-lit hall. Like I figured the place was unfurnished. Nikko sniffed fastidiously.

'I shall be glad to get back to the Big Apple,' he told the cobwebs.

'That's the worst of these provincial assignments,' I told him.

He opened up the door at the far end of the hall and we went through into a long, bare room, empty except for several chairs, a rough trestle table and a couple of camp beds. There was a massive stone fireplace on the right-hand side and French doors on the left.

It had once been a very fine room and in fact the fireplace wall was covered with rococo-style panelling but time, neglect and damp had made a melancholy thing of it.

But I wasn't here for the decor and I walked over quickly and got my back to the fireplace. Nikko stood and looked at me mournfully, like he wished he'd thought of it first.

'Just to make it more fair,' I said. 'When your friend arrives.'

169

Nikko gave another of his jackal smiles, revealing his strong yellow teeth.

There were lines of humour at the corners of his mouth now.

'Don't you trust anybody,' he told the two bare ceiling bulbs suspended by scarlet flex from elaborate carved roses.

'I've been around a long time,' I said. 'I aim to go on being around.'

Nikko blinked sleepily, stepping back toward the far wall. His head was cocked on one side, as though he were listening for something.

'It seems fair enough,' he said reasonably.

Quick, nervous steps crossed the parquet in the next room and the far door was suddenly flung open. Framed in the dim oblong was a familiar figure. He moved down the room toward me, his lips opening in a tight smile.

'Well, well,' I said. 'Mr Holt. It figures. First Albert. Now you. Is Mr Harrison hiding in the next room.'

The estate manager shook his head. He looked like Zachary Scott on his day off with his snappy blue blazer and pale cream military-style trousers. Except that Zachary wasn't around any more.

Holt put out his hand and came farther down the room toward me.

'That's far enough,' I said.

Nikko shook his head disapprovingly at the dapper figure of Holt.

'A dumb play, Mr Holt.'

The estate manager turned a startled face over his shoulder.

'I don't get it,' he said. 'I thought we were all friends here. We got to combine in this crisis.'

Nikko shook his head.

'The crisis is ours, not Mr Faraday's. He's on the other side. Or hadn't you noticed?'

I was getting to like him more by the minute. Which was surprising under the circumstances. Holt bit his lip, turning his glance back to me.

'But haven't you explained the circumstances? With more than a million dollars at stake . . . Surely, we've got to join forces.'

I shook my head, feeling the weight of the Smith-Wesson in the nylon holster.

'I don't know what you're talking about,' I said.

Gary Holt's black patent leather hair, Ronald Colman mustache and the white teeth in the frank smile seemed a little tarnished now and he no longer had the David Niven image. There was a thin glaze of perspiration on his forehead.

'Brown knew where the stuff was,' he said somewhat desperately. 'I thought you may have come across that information. We have a problem. Time, mainly . . .'

'I know,' I said. 'The people in the East are

171

getting impatient. Even Nikko here has shown some concern.'

Holt shook his head.

'This is serious, Mr Faraday. We simply got to pool our resources.'

I grinned.

'You're not threatening me, I hope. I don't threaten easily.'

Holt looked offended.

'Good heavens, no, Mr Faraday. I regard you as an ally.'

'Like Mr Brown,' I said. 'If he knew where the stuff was why did Albert drop him?'

Holt bit his lip again. He was getting pretty good at it. Nikko had a bored look on his face. He was leaning casually against the wall in rear of Holt but my eyes never left his hands. He was like a coiled steel spring and I didn't aim to let him get the drop on me.

'I had a phone call while you were away,' he told Holt suddenly. 'It was Mr Grimaldi. He's becoming impatient. He's sent some more people out.'

Holt turned white. He swallowed once or twice but no words came initially.

'Albert was a fool,' he said savagely. 'That's why we got this trouble. We had a nice racket going. We acted as a channel, merely. There was little or no risk until the New York Jewellers' Association started putting heavy muscle on us.'

His voice was offended, like he was talking

about some unfair trade practice. I would have been amused at any other time. But not tonight. There was a bad atmosphere; things didn't sit right. I wasn't worried about Holt. He was an amateur. And Nikko was a danger I could face. It was something else I couldn't put my finger on.

'You made a foul-up all round,' I told Holt. 'Relaying that message from Albert saying he'd run Brown back from Cocos safely.'

Holt had a blank, shuttered face.

'I don't get it.'

I shook my head.

'You've only been firing on two cylinders throughout. I couldn't pin you at first but the Albert story smelt as high as a fish-dock. You said Albert waited until he saw Brown walk back to his parked car. My brain was slowed down because of brawl-damage at the time but it started working again.

'Both you and Albert probably thought Brown came out with Dad Corcoran from the mainland. In actual fact he came on a charter boat from Bridport Inlet, which is over eighty miles down the coast. So Brown couldn't possibly have had his car parked where Albert said he was.'

The silence that followed was long and heavy. Holt set his jaw firmly and Nikko just went on staring at me. The whole thing was obviously immaterial to him.

'What about Harrison?' I said. 'Is he in on

173

the racket?'

Holt shook his head.

'Don't be ridiculous, Mr Faraday. What we are doing is peanuts to him. He was the greatest front.'

He turned pink, the perspiration streaming off his forehead as he stared first at me and then at Nikko.

'Good heavens, I could get fired if this got out.'

This time Nikko laughed out loud. He was just too late to beat me to it.

'You could get dead too.' I told him. 'I'm telling you the truth. I don't know where the stuff is.'

In the hush that followed I heard the sound of an engine in the lane outside, then another. Nikko and Holt were standing so still they looked like something out of a wax museum. I took out the Smith-Wesson, put it in my right-hand trouser pocket, kept my hand on the butt. Nikko didn't try to stop me. Holt didn't even notice.

Doors slammed outside and heavy footsteps sounded over the gravel. There seemed to be a lot of them. Holt jerked his head at me.

'You didn't bring the police?'

'Grow up, Mr Holt,' Nikko gritted.

A boot crashed against the French windows, making them rattle. Holt went forward jerkily, his fingers fumbling at the bolts. A big form in a dark, sober suit came into sight in the shadowy garden beyond. Nikko's eyes held mine for a long moment. There was a strange, misty expression in them. It was the look of one pro to another; a sort of Roman salute, if that wasn't being too fanciful.

The man who came forward into the room was more elderly than middle-aged, with a frosty mane of hair that fell over his ears. His voice was low and soft so that one had to strain to hear it and the dark pools of his eyes revealed no emotion whatsoever. The atmosphere he gave off was so deadly I kept my hand in my pocket.

The old man nodded frostily at Holt, gave a regretful look across at Nikko. The big man drew himself up like he'd been struck.

'Mr Grimaldi sent us. You know why we're here.'

Nikko nodded. Holt seemed like someone had slammed him in the gut. The white-haired man's eyes speared me to the wall.

'Who's this?'

'No-one,' Nikko said quickly. 'Just an old friend from way back.'

The old man looked at me sharply, his face remote and impersonal.

'What's he got to do with this?'

Nikko shook his head.

'Nothing,' he said before anyone else could speak.

His eyes avoided Holt's sick face. The man with the dead eyes glanced at me casually.

175

'We got no quarrel with you, mister. Beat it.'

I stared at Nikko for a long moment, gave him a slight bow. Holt was having a choking fit. I went on out through the French window quickly, before he cracked. The garden seemed to be full of big, broad-shouldered men in dark suits. They gave way as though by some invisible command, their eyes focused on the three men in the room beyond.

I found I was sweating when I got in the seat of the Buick and it took three pulls before the engine fired. Then I was rocking back down the driveway. I was almost at the end of the lane before the shooting began.

CHAPTER EIGHTEEN

1

I drove on steadily for about five miles before I pulled in to a layby. I lit a cigarette and felt better then. My brain had taken a battering tonight but I was beginning to think straight. All my interest was concentrated on Reardon and the girl; on his lonely trip to Cocos Island from a point so far from the location.

Over a million dollars of syndicate money had gone astray, that was for sure. But was Harrison mixed up in it or had Holt been speaking the truth? Or could a third party have been concerned? If Harrison was the Mr Big who was handling the West coast pipeline for the New York syndicate I'd hardly have much chance of nailing him. But something had been worrying at the back of my mind all evening and I went on sweating away at it while I finished off my cigarette.

I knew the general outline but there were still some holes in the story. Nikko had said he had nothing to do with shooting at Alex Prosser. What's more, I believed him. One had a certainty about things like that. And, as I said, Nikko was the sort of man who would have told me if it were true. Those characters were hardly worried about the law or what a solitary P.I. might say or do. They'd already proved that with Reardon.

I was surprised that Holt had come out into the open like that. But if the East was on his neck he had no choice. And both Holt and Nikko had initially been convinced that I knew where the diamonds were hidden. It was obvious now that I'd disabused Nikko of that notion. He'd never have given me an out otherwise.

I wouldn't be seeing Nikko or Holt again, that was for sure. The syndicate had lost patience. Question was, would they go on with the search. Or was there someone else in there, hiding among the pattern in the carpet, that I hadn't figured on? My, we are getting Jamesian tonight, Mike, I told myself. And I wasn't talking about Jesse. It was evident my sense of humour was coming back. What was left of it anyway.

I took the Smith-Wesson out my pocket and put it back in the shoulder-holster. I drove on again after a few more minutes, still teasing things out. Could Reardon have hidden something somewhere for his sister or the authorities to find? Not necessarily the diamonds but a pointer to their whereabouts. And why had he wanted to cross to Cocos that night?

The more I drove and the more I worried about it, the bigger the tangle seemed. Certainly a syndicate member had absconded with the loot; that much was now clear and the idea had been reinforced by Nikko earlier tonight. So it had to be somewhere or the syndicate wouldn't still be searching. They had to enforce discipline or they couldn't stay in business.

I remembered Lionel Prosser and the *Glory B* then. His dropping on me like a ton of concrete. There was a faint misty something at the back of my brain that was growing more substantial and solid with every mile the Buick's wheels took me. I got out my large-scale and glanced at it by the dashboard light, altered course at the next junction. I started making time toward Bridport Inlet.

It was a fine, moonlight night and I burned up the tarmac. I stopped at a diner on the way and got outside a steak and green salad while I continued mulling over the situation. I knew now who'd knocked over Brown-Reardon, it was true, and I'd repaid the debt. But I was still far from solving what he'd given his life for. He'd gone out to Cocos for something and the *Glory B* was the vessel involved.

I was even beginning to connect up Alex Prosser; I switched off my mind and took my cup of coffee into the public phone booth in the dinette. I'd become unglued if I went on like that. I reached Stella first time off and filled her in on the situation. I waited while she took notes, ignoring the sullen looks of a black-haired truckie who was waiting outside.

'You'd better tell McGiver,' I said. 'He may be able to locate what's left of Nikko and Holt. He could also try L.A. International. They may pick up the characters responsible before they fly out. But whether they can make it stick is another matter.'

I gave Stella a description of white-hair and asked her to turn over Nikko's Colt to the police, with some plausible excuse. There was no point in hanging on to it now. And the barrel rifling might match up with some other kill we didn't know about.

'Kathy all right?' I said.

'She's asleep,' Stella said. 'Anything else you want me to do?'

'Not really,' I said. 'Just be there.'

Stella smiled. Don't ask me how I knew. I could sense it in her voice.

'I'm always here, Mike,' she said softly.

I changed the conversation quickly, got on to a less dangerous tack. I told her where I was going, what I intended.

'Look after yourself,' she said.

I rang off and got out the booth. The truckie was making aggressive noises.

'You're a highly sequacious sort of fellow,' I said.

'What does that mean?' he said suspiciously.

'Look it up,' I told him.

I was still smiling when I ordered my second cup of coffee.

180

2

It was around ten o'clock when I got to Bridport Inlet and parked the Buick halfway between Prosser's boatyard and the boardwalk restaurant where I'd had coffee the other morning. It seemed years ago now. There was mauve and green neon pricking the dusk and the chain of yellow-globed lamps round the foreshore made the place momentarily look like an old photograph of Monte Carlo as it might have been in the twenties.

Only there were no grand hotels and casinos in the darkness beyond the range of the lamps. I walked on back down, keeping to the soft sand of the beach, listening to the faint susurrance of the waves as they broke in a line of creamy white where the moonlight bleached the water; listening to an old jazz tune someone was playing on a car-radio; and avoiding the spots where couples strolled hand in hand; and older people walked their dogs.

It was just the craziest of hunches, sparked off by my encounter with Lionel Prosser. Maybe the *Glory B* wasn't even moored here tonight in which case my journey had been wasted. But I had nothing else to lose and now that Holt and Nikko had been taken out I had nowhere else to go.

If nothing turned up tonight then the million dollars-plus worth of diamonds—if they existed—would have to remain missing.

Together with the elusive Mr Big. And that went against the grain.

I was up alongside the pier now, with its chain of lights and I remembered then that Prosser had said it was a private set-up and that the entire structure belonged to the brothers. But though the public were barred at night they couldn't very well stop boat owners from coming and going to their vessels.

I went up the wooden staircase that led from the beach and found a warning notice and an iron chain hooked across at the top. But it took only a second to step over it and there were unlikely to be any alarms out here. No-one on the boats themselves would bother about me strolling around unless I did something odd to arouse their suspicions. My main problem was likely to be locating the vessel and I hoped there'd be enough light for that purpose.

The tide was on the turn; neither fully in nor fully out and it sounded loud and magnified as I walked on down, the metal decking giving out heavy reverberations beneath my size nines. It took me longer than I figured. The pier was empty but my imagination conjured up dark figures on the decks of the boats moored in long strings alongside.

There were lamps on steel poles set at intervals along the metal railings of the pier and presumably these were kept on all night both for the benefit of boat owners and to dissuade thieves. I started out by trying the place where the *Glory B* had been moored before. Presumably Prosser, as owner of the pier, would have priority for his own vessels and maybe a regular mooring.

But there was no sign of the big sea-going vessel where she'd tied up last time and I went farther down, going into a more dimly-lit area between two lamps. I could hear conversation and radios now so I knew some of the crews were aboard the moored yachts and cruisers. I walked carefully then, making as little noise as possible, the Smith-Wesson a hard, compact pressure against my shoulder muscles.

I realised I'd fired it only three times on the case. Which was a pretty low average for me. I gave my teeth a brief airing in the semi-darkness, enjoying the warm salt flow of the air from the sea across my battered face, conscious too of the faint twinge that my leg was still giving out.

A couple of yards farther on I came across a big white board screwed to the railings on the leeward side of the pier which proclaimed Private Moorings for Prosser craft. This seemed more like it and as it was just under a lamp I went a ways down the short wooden ladder that was set in the gap between two sections of metal railing. The protecting chains had been unhooked and shivered slightly in the breeze which had sprung up, making occasional chinking noises against the uprights.

There were some dock lights set into the piling down here and by their glow and that of the moon I could see pretty clearly. The *Glory B* was outboard a large, sea-going yacht lying at the foot of the ladder. There was light coming from its hatchway so I knew the owners were aboard. The yacht was rocking with the tide but I managed to step over without making any undue noise.

I went across quickly, avoiding the open hatch and got up the short companionway to the *Glory B*. If the hatch entrance here was locked I would have a problem. I might have broken one of the coachroof windows if the vessel had been lying in a secluded position but that was impossible here. I was sweating now, the rivulets drying almost immediately with the warmth of the breeze.

In the event it was an anti-climax. The hatch was open and smells of stale cooking came up from the galley below. I hoped there would be battery lighting aboard. That was something I hadn't figured either because the tweendecks area was dark. Usually the electrics on a boat like this ran off a dynamo operated by the engines. But a vessel like this would surely have secondary lighting for port work.

I went down the companionway into the warm interior, listening to the creaking of timbers and the soft slap of water, a nerve twitching in my cheek. If I drew a blank in the saloon I'd try the wheelhouse. Though what I was looking for I didn't really know. Some evidence of Reardon's presence aboard. Like I said it was the wildest of hunches but it was all I had.

I shot a glance at my watch in the moonlight coming through the nearest coachroof window. It was already after ten-thirty. I'd be here all night at this rate. I tried the brass switch inside the saloon door. A couple of flush-fitting lamps set in the deckhead winked on.

I went over quickly and drew the curtains on the starboard side, that nearest the big yacht next door. There was no sign of the fracas I'd had with Lionel Prosser in here. I guessed the boatyard staff had seen to that the same afternoon before the hire-party turned up.

I spent the next quarter hour in a careful search of the lockers and cupboards. There was nothing in them that there shouldn't have been and that was no surprise. Then I turned my attention to the shelving that ran along behind the padded banquettes either side the cabin table.

Like always they were full of cheap paperbacks and clothbound editions of novelettes. But there were a few weightier things, including some books of navigation charts that Prosser or his clients might need to consult down here on cosy evenings rather than in the more austere surroundings of the wheelhouse.

I went through the first three, looking for scribbled notations. The fourth was a large volume, bound in black cloth. From the gold lettering on the spine I saw it was a collection of charts giving details of Californian coastal waters. I took it down and opened it up, flipped through it casually.

As I did so a white envelope fluttered to the cabin floor. I bent down to pick it up. Scribbled in ink at the top left-hand side was the instruction; To be opened in the event of my death. It was addressed to Kathy Reardon at a location in West L.A.

My fingers were an inch away from it when the roof fell in for the second time. I went out as definitively as hand-made fudge.

CHAPTER NINETEEN

1

The rumble in my ears translated itself into the low vibration of diesel engines; the shivering pattern in front of my face oak planking seen close up. I felt salt wind on my face and blinked back to consciousness, aware of a blinding pain at the back of my head.

'He's around,' a man said.

A girl's voice replied but it was so low I couldn't make out its import. I reached out my right hand, found I could flex my fingers. The man's voice laughed then.

'He must have a skull like concrete.'

I didn't bother looking for the Smith-Wesson. I knew it wouldn't be there. I rolled over, found I was in one piece. I was lying on the small bridge-wing of the *Glory B*'s wheelhouse. Leastways, I imagined I was still aboard the same vessel. We were just clearing the harbour of Bridport Inlet because I could see the red-painted lighthouse slide past on the starboard side, with its complement of winking and fixed lights.

I looked around, saw a face from the dead. Holt's ashen features seemed like those of a ventriloquist's doll someone had sewn loosely atop a body that didn't belong to it. The body itself was just a collection of old clothes that slewed and slithered with the slight bucking movement the *Glory B* was making. I realised then he was tied into an angle of the wheelhouse with strong marine cord.

It was pure will that was keeping him conscious. The tattered, bloody mess that had been his immaculate blazer, had at least three bullet holes punched through it.

'It's a bad scene,' he said in a toneless voice.

'You can say that again,' I said. 'What's holding you up?'

He shook his head feebly, blood crusted on his lips.

'I'll give you anything if you'll get me out of this.'

I heard a cracked laugh then, realised it was my own voice.

'I'll have a job to get myself out.'

'How right you are, Mr Faraday,' the girl's voice said.

I admired a magnificent pair of legs that sauntered over the planking toward me. My eyes went out of focus again for a minute or two and when I had them under control the girl had gone back into the wheelhouse. I was fighting to stay awake. Holt was either a good deal tougher than I'd given him credit for or the wounds looked worse than they really were.

'How did you get away from Mr Grimaldi's boys?' I said.

I was making conversation really but I had nothing better to do until I could get nerve and sinew together. And I wasn't quite ready for that yet.

Holt shook his head, his eyes closed now.

'They left me for dead,' he said. 'I went out cold. That was what saved me.'

'It's a tough world,' I said. 'The league was too big for you. What happened to Nikko?'

'He fought it out.' Holt said, his eyes open again now. 'They had to put enough lead in him to sink the QE2.'

I digested the information in silence.

'He was a pro,' I told the wind and the waves.

'He got two of them before he went,' Holt said with satisfaction. 'I was trying to get back to Cocos. I remember arriving at Bridport Inlet. I must have passed out on the pier.'

The footsteps were back again now. I rolled over, got my spine up against a bulkhead, stared at the tall girl with chestnut hair.

'Miss Diane Morris if memory serves me correctly.'

The girl looked at me contemptuously.

'You remember good.'

'This is a bit out of the way for you, isn't it?' I said.

The tall number shook her head.

'Not with the sort of money we're playing for.'

'I thought waiting table was more in your

line,' I said.

The girl glanced at me thoughtfully.

'It was a good front,' she said. 'Close to the boatyard. And I had to be careful. There was a jealous wife involved.'

I didn't get it but my attention was wavering again now as I fought to keep conscious. Whoever had sapped me had done the job real good.

'What about Holt?' I said. 'He needs medical attention badly.'

The girl shook her head. She glanced briefly from Holt's ashen face to me.

'He won't suffer long. We were watching the *Glory B* when we saw the cabin lights go on. Then Holt turned up. It was neatly timed. You're both going over the side. Why do you think we're taking the boat out tonight?'

'That's nice,' I said. 'You've been seeing too many re-runs of Key Largo on TV.'

'Nice enough,' the man's voice said.

He had to be there, of course, in the wheelhouse because the vessel couldn't run itself but I felt surprise. That showed how badly beat-up I was.

He shoved his head out through the sliding glass window then. He was a tall, broad-shouldered character with black hair. I didn't recognise him. Not Mr Big, surely. We'd see. Either way it seemed academic now. If this was a one-way trip. There were still a number of pieces I needed. I'd like to check, just for the record.

I noticed the girl had my Smith-Wesson. I didn't know whether she knew how to use it. And I didn't aim to find out in my present condition. But she looked an amateur. If there was to be an out that seemed the only way.

She glanced casually at Holt and me and then back at the man who was steering the *Glory B* into a light swell. It was still a fine moonlight night and any other time the sparkle on the wavelets would have been great. But not tonight. Not under these circumstances.

'How long will it take, Leo?'

The big man shook his dark head amiably.

'Why don't you give him my address, honey?'

Diane Morris looked at him without resentment.

'I didn't think it mattered now.'

The man carefully steering the *Glory B* turned down the corners of his mouth.

'You have a lot to learn, Diane. It's not over until it's over. Remember the man who once sold the lion's skin . . . ?'

'I don't know what you're talking about,' the girl said petulantly.

'You wouldn't, honey,' I said. 'It's Shakespeare.'

The big man grinned.

'That's right, Faraday. Pity you had to get in the way like this.'

'Just what I was thinking,' I said. 'Where do you intend to put us off?'

I glanced at Holt. He was either dead or passed out.

The man called Leo shifted his attention back to the illuminated compass card in front of him.

'When we get halfway across,' he said. 'I got to watch the tides, you see. Too many bodies along this coast will attract too much attention.'

'To Cocos?' I said.

Leo shrugged.

'Maybe,' he said casually.

'What was in the envelope?' I said.

The big man steering the vessel so meticulously exchanged glances with Diane Morris.

'Navigational aids, let's say. Something that will considerably improve my life-style.'

'Sounds good,' I said.

'It is good, Mr Faraday,' he said.

We were just getting to that interesting point in the conversation when I passed out again.

2

When I came around the motors had been throttled back and the *Glory B* was rolling a little more to the increased swell. The moon was partly obscured by cloud but there was enough light for me to see that all land had disappeared. I still had a headache but I felt a lot stronger and my brain was working properly.

I knew Leo and the girl would have a problem now. I'd have to wait until they started to put us over the side. Somebody's attention might stray at that moment. But it was going to be hard waiting for the point of no return. I'd have to pretend I was a good deal more damaged than I was. So I lay still, feeling my strength returning, watching from under half-closed eyelids.

Leo was still steering, of course, but I could see the girl's feet a little farther along the deck. She was obviously seated on one of the slatted wooden benches fitted to the guard rail for the use of passengers on pleasure trips. She was too far away for me to do anything and she had the gun. So that was out.

I quickly checked on Holt. He was still sitting slumped in the corner, held up by the ropes. It was impossible to see whether he was dead or alive but it looked like the bleeding had stopped. I wouldn't find any help there. Like always, Mike, I told myself, it's up to you. The window of the wheelhouse slid back then and Leo poked his head out.

'Another ten minutes,' he told the girl curtly.

Despite the dimness of the moonlight he didn't miss anything. His head swivelled toward me as menacingly as a battleship's gun-turret. I saw then he had the muzzle of a big cannon resting on the ledge of the wheelhouse window. He certainly wasn't taking any chances. I'd been wise in my precautions.

'So you're awake again, Faraday,' he said softly.

'Briefly, it appears,' I said.

He smiled sardonically.

'You have a gallows sense of humour.'

I did my best to give a shrug.

'I work with the material I got.'

While we were making with the patter, I wondered how he'd known I was awake again. Maybe it was something so trivial and yet so important as the moonlight glinting on my eyeballs. Sounds like something out of a B-horror movie, Mike, I told myself. I looked at the girl, making sure to stay motionless like I was still half-conscious.

It was then I saw Holt's eyes flicker briefly. So he wasn't dead. Unless it was just a muscular reflex. The girl got up from the seat and came on down the deck toward me. I braced myself to grab her round the ankles. It was a crazy play but it was the best I could think of. Fortunately, I didn't try. Firstly, because the girl seemed to have an instinct about such things and took a wide circuit to the wheelhouse where Leo stood at the open window.

And secondly, and most importantly, I could now see by the strengthening light of the moon

194

that he must have lashed the wheel on course and had the big cannon levelled steadily at my chest.

'You're old friends, then,' I said.

The girl laughed. It made a harsh, metallic sound out here above the fretful rushing of the waves.

'Three years,' she said. 'No harm in telling you now. That's how long Leo and me have been lovers. And if it wasn't for that blue-rinsed old woman he's married to, we'd have made it legit long before now.'

'Tough,' I said mildly.

'I got the job at the restaurant as a front and so I could be on hand,' the girl said. 'We were cleaning up plenty cash and I was helping out with the courier work.'

She didn't say what she was talking about and she didn't have to. I knew the score and she knew it too.

'It was going great until that son-of-a-bitch screwed it up,' Leo said bitterly. 'He brought the heat on all of us. Plus the law and then Reardon, There was a little creep called Carter who decided to go into business for himself by lighting out with over a million dollars' worth of the syndicate's diamonds. Albert got to him, but he escaped, badly wounded. Before he died, he passed on to Reardon the details of where he'd stashed the diamonds. Leastways, that's my reading of it.'

'You were lucky Mr Grimaldi didn't lean on

you,' I said.

Leo shook his head.

'No-one knows about me,' he said. 'Except a select few. I just provide a service. I'm around here at Bridport Inlet. Like I'm part of the furniture.'

'So you're Mr Big?' I said.

He joined in the girl's laughter.

'So far as there is one. It's a vast company, Mr Faraday. All sorts of different compartments. Watertight boxes, you might say. With one box not knowing what's going on in the next one. And much, much safer.'

'So what went wrong?' I said.

I eased my cramped position slightly against the bulkhead. Leo's gun swivelled almost as fast as my movement. He wasn't missing a trick. I decided to be comatose from now on. Until the time came to really move.

Leo shrugged again.

'A combination of things, really. I admit I was greedy. I'd milked my firm dry. And I had to have more.'

'The lady's expensive is she?' I said.

Diane Morris' eyes had dangerous glints in them. Leo shot me a crooked grin.

'Aren't they all?' he said.

'So you knew who I was when I turned up at the restaurant?' I said.

'We pegged you right from the start,' Leo said. 'That was the beauty of our system. In a small place like Bridport Inlet strangers get

196

noticed. You can soon pick them out from the genuine tourists. And we had advance notice of your coming.'

That set my brain-cogs working. The pain in my head was receding now but the ache in my leg was coming back. I should have to watch that. Maybe I ought to register for that old people's home Stella kept talking about. I had a sudden vision of her phoning McGiver. None of that would help now. Not out here, maybe more than twenty miles from shore.

I couldn't be certain but I guessed Leo's eventual destination would be Cocos. I hadn't entirely scrubbed Harrison from my list but there could be another angle I hadn't figured. One that Reardon had stumbled on.

'What was really in that envelope?' I said.

Leo smiled triumphantly.

'The stuff that dreams are made of, Mr Faraday. It's been a perfect set-up and it all fell into my lap by accident. I been searching for something Reardon may have left ever since that creep Albert fouled things up. I staked out the boat and you did the work for us.'

'I'm still curious,' I said.

The girl gave Leo a warning glance but he went on casually just the same.

'A brief note to Reardon's sister to notify the police. Plus a map reference which it didn't take me longer than ten minutes to work out from the right coastal chart. That's why we're

197

here.'

'So you're Mr Mini-Big,' I said. 'I'm disappointed. I don't even know your name.'

The girl bit her lip.

'Let's leave it like that, Mr Faraday,' she said quickly.

The big man nodded.

'I think the lady's right,' he told the bow-wave.

He shook his head slowly.

'I'm not really Mr Big, Faraday. And you never thought so either. I'm just a little man who's getting what's due to him. There is no Mr Big, certainly not Harrison. Sure, there's a Mr Big in New York. And another in charge of Southern California. But no-one knows who they really are. And no-one's ever likely to know.'

He moved back into the wheelhouse and the engines throbbed more strongly again.

'I think we've done enough talking,' he said through the open window.

I looked at the girl. With her white raincoat and knotted silk scarf she looked like something out of the Yachtsman's Delight. Or whatever they call it. She sat down again, holding my Smith-Wesson casually in her lap, on a bench that ran up to the wheelhouse just to the right of where Holt lay slumped. He seemed dead already, his dark hair whipped by the wind across his closed eyes.

We went on like that for perhaps another

198

quarter of an hour. Then the sound of the motors died away as the man Leo shut off and we were wallowing in the pale moonlight in an eerie silence. The wheelhouse door slid back and he re-appeared. He was enormously tall and his gaunt, sardonic face vaguely reminded me of someone I knew.

He came down the deck toward me as the girl sat erect, the Smith-Wesson high and ready for use now. It was then that I saw a faint crack in the after hatchway cover that shouldn't have been there. Or maybe it was a trick of the moonlight. The man Leo bent over me, the pistol close to my head.

'I think this is as far as you go, Mr Faraday,' he said.

I reached up for the rail, tried to claw myself upright but I'd left it too late. An iron hand was at my collar, kept me pinned in a crouching position as the enormous cannon came closer.

'What are you waiting for?' the girl said.

We were poised like that, a frozen frame from a movie, the shattering crash of the explosion a few split-fractions away when a streak of silver tore the sky diagonally like a split in a piece of paper. The tall man made a gurgling sound and the cannon hit the deck and bounced into the sea, the waves noiselessly receiving it.

Diane Morris had the Smith-Wesson up when a dead man came to life for the second time, the blood-caked form of Holt jack-knifing, his flailing fist smashing the girl back into the wheelhouse.

The echo of the shot cracked across the water as a vast figure erupted on deck from the open hatchway amidships. I nose-dived across the planking, ducking beneath the pistol barrel as the girl fought to get the weapon to bear.

CHAPTER TWENTY

1

The gun went off again, with deafening effect at such close range. Blue smoke enveloped the girl's head and then I heard bone crack as I forced her arm back. She screamed and the gun clattered down. I put my foot on it, ignoring the girl as she went on screaming.

I kept Holt from collapsing, watching the silhouette of the dark man against the moonlit sea shimmer. He seemed to be taking a long time to die, supporting himself by a stanchion and retching into the waves below. The long barbed steel shaft fired by the spear-gun protruded several inches beyond his chest as he sagged at the rail.

Alex Prosser's face was a bronzed image of pain and hatred as he came down the deck, the planking trembling beneath his massive weight. His right hand, casual and lethal, side-swiped Diane Morris, cutting off the screaming. She went into the superstructure and passed out cold. I got my free hand beneath her as she fell, protecting her head from further damage.

The tall dark man was dead and diving over the side when Prosser got to him. He lowered him with curious gentleness to the deck. He stood, head bowed for a few seconds, low whimpering noises coming out his mouth. Then he bent and went through the big man's pockets, like no-one else was there. The *Glory B* carried on rocking to the tide.

I leaned back against the bulkhead, cradling Holt's limp body, feeling old and tired and half-dead myself. Prosser had the white envelope out now, peered uncertainly at the contents.

'What is it?' I said.

Prosser shook his head slowly, like he was coming out of an anaesthetic.

'Forgive me, Mr Faraday. I had to do it. He would have killed you otherwise. I didn't think things would have gone this far.'

'Don't apologise,' I said. 'You saved my life.'

Prosser was kneeling by my side now. He took Holt's body from me, cradling it with amazing tenderness for such a huge man. He cut the ropes with a big jack-knife he produced from somewhere. He put Holt down on the deck, covering him with a length of tarpaulin. He knelt again, head bent to the estate manager's chest.

'He's still breathing,' he said. 'He might have a chance if we can get him to shore.'

He turned back to me.

'You'd better have some of this.'

I coughed as the raw spirit trickled down my throat but I was coming alive again. I put the Smith-Wesson back in my shoulder-holster, lit a cigarette with slightly unsteady hands. Prosser was still kneeling, watching me with calm anxiety.

'You did real good, Mr Faraday,' he said slowly. 'You'd best tie her up before she comes around. That one's a real killer.'

I took the rope he passed me and did like he said, rocking now as the bow of the *Glory B* swung with the tide, trying not to look at the thing on the deck; the bloodied form of Holt; and the crumpled figure of the girl. This made the finale of Macbeth look like pretty tame stuff.

'Where did you come from?' I said.

Prosser got up then, his heavy face tragic in the moonlight. He licked dry lips, taking the flask from me.

'I was hiding in the sail locker. I been keeping an eye on the *Glory B* for some while. I was convinced the guy who tried to kill me would come back. I didn't think it would end up like this.'

'You set me up,' I said.

Alex Prosser shook his massive head.

'For the love of God, Mr Faraday, don't ever say that. I had a few crazy ideas about this set-up. I thought you might smoke someone out if you kept rooting around. Like I said you did just great.'

'I still don't get it,' I said. 'What was in that envelope? Reardon left it for his sister. Leo said something about a map reference.'

Prosser nodded.

'That's right. It gives a geographical location. What's the point of it? I couldn't hear properly back there.'

I gave him a long, hard look, supporting myself by one hand against the deckhouse. I was afraid I might fall down otherwise.

'That piece of paper should lead us to more than a million dollars' worth of illicit diamonds. A little cache that quite a few have already died for. A good thing you didn't let Leo fall overboard or no-one would ever have known.'

Prosser's massive features looked blank in the moonlight. He stared grimly down at the deck of the *Glory B*.

'Where was that location?' I said.

'Difficult to be absolutely certain without more detailed checking,' he said. 'But my rough guess is somewhere near Cocos Island.'

He shook himself and came to life. He slid open the wheelhouse door and went inside. A few seconds later the interior light blinked on and the powerful engines vibrated the hull. The bow turned swiftly as he spun the wheel and then we were bucking back on course toward the shore. I finished tying the cord round the girl's ankles; she was still out, breathing heavily through her nose. I stood for a moment looking at the calmness and beauty of the moon on the sea, like something out of an old Gustave Dore engraving. The taste of salt and the rough caress of the wind on my face felt good.

I went in the wheelhouse, leaving the door open so I could check on our passengers; one unconscious, one dead, one maybe dying. It was difficult to make out Prosser's expression as he stood with head bowed, studying the compass card. I was astonished to see something glisten on his cheeks in the dim overhead light.

'Who was he?' I said. 'The guy the girl called Leo.'

Prosser kept his face averted. His voice was cracked and trembling now.

'I had to do it, Mr Faraday. He would have killed you and Holt. He was cheating on his wife; and I suspect he's taken hundreds of thousands of dollars out my company.'

I stared at him in astonishment.

'Who was he?' I repeated gently.

Prosser's voice was so low I could hardly make out his reply.

'He was my brother,' he said.

2

There was a long silence between us, made heavier and more forbidding by the throbbing of the *Glory B*'s engines.

'I don't know what to say,' I told him. 'Except I'm sorry.'

Prosser kept on shaking his head wearily.

'Don't try, Mr Faraday. It's all too complicated.'

He looked at me fiercely, straightening up at the wheel.

'One thing made me see red. I couldn't let him kill you, of course. But I was certain of something else. That's what made me pull the trigger when I might have warned him.'

'What was that?' I said, feathering out blue smoke through the port wheelhouse window where it was chopped to segments by the rising breeze.

Prosser's face was as heavily set as a death-mask.

'He was the guy who tried to kill me that night I disturbed him at the wheelhouse,' he said. 'I found a pistol in his desk at the yard. One chamber had been fired. That pistol went over the side tonight. I been thinking about it a lot. Leo was wearing some sort of fancy get-up but there was something familiar about him in the muzzle-flash. He thought I might have recognised him. And he couldn't afford that. So he tried to take me out. I guess he took off without stopping when he saw me fall.'

There was great bitterness in his voice.

'Imagine that, Mr Faraday. A guy who would kill his own brother in cold blood.'

He gave me a twisted smile.

'Like me.'

I stared at him incredulously, shook my head.

206

'Not like you, Alex. You killed him in hot blood. And for all those very good reasons you've already enumerated. What worries me is not the police but the impact on the family. How are you going to explain this to his wife? Or live with it afterward?'

Prosser's eyes were calm and assured now.

'I'll live with that, Mike,' he said steadily.

Like always he'd suddenly remembered we were on first-name terms.

'Things haven't been well there for a long time.'

He glanced out the wheelhouse window.

'And then there's the girl. She was Leo's mistress. I've seen them together on a few occasions and I was told things from time to time. That makes a difference to a woman. I guess Lottie will forgive me when this mess comes out in court. After all, Leo was cheating the whole family when he was cooking the accounts. I spent the last few nights going through the books. Leo wasn't the accountant for nothing.'

I just went on smoking without saying anything. I guessed the family would live with it. Like Alex had said he'd saved two lives tonight. If Holt lived, that is.

'Some things I don't get,' I said. 'Maybe the police will come up with the answers. Reardon was going out to Cocos to investigate the syndicate's rackets. Probably to recover the diamonds. He made the mistake of going to the public jetty where Albert was on duty. Maybe Reardon already felt his life was running out. So as an insurance he left that navigational reference among the charts in the hope that it would find its way to his sister one day.'

Prosser nodded, his forehead corrugated with thought. He was in command of himself again now.

'That must have been it, Mr Faraday. If this is the key to stolen diamonds how would he have found out?'

'One of the syndicate's couriers decided to go into business for himself,' I said. 'The same people who killed Reardon had already caught up with him. He was dying when he told Reardon where he'd stashed the stuff.'

Prosser nodded.

'So the people on Cocos were in the thick of it.'

'Some of them,' I said. 'We'll never tie Martin Harrison in, that's for sure. And it's by no means certain he had anything to do with it. Even a million's small beer for his league.'

'So my brother was part of it,' Prosser said.

'Looks like it,' I told him. 'The girl was expensive; he'd milked off the company's funds so he turned to the pipeline.'

Prosser's eyes were puzzled again.

'But why so far up the coast?'

I shrugged, watching the moonlit water slide by through the open window.

'Maybe the people on Cocos were becoming careless. The mainland settlement opposite there is a very small place. Perhaps they needed another base of operations to avoid arousing suspicion. Bridport Inlet was ideal. Your boatyard would have been perfect. They could have shipped stuff to and fro, posing as tourist trade without any local comment. And your brother could have run the stuff himself without anyone ever knowing.'

'Sounds plausible,' Prosser said.

'What I don't get,' I said, 'is why your brother should have to break into the *Glory B*. Surely he could have come aboard any time and searched for what Reardon had left behind without arousing suspicion. I had your other brother Lionel pegged for that role when he downed me in the cabin.'

Prosser's face cleared.

'I can help you there, Mike. It wouldn't have been as simple as that. The *Glory B* is my favourite vessel and my own personal property. I even sleep aboard at the pier some nights. The cabin and wheelhouse are always kept locked and I have the only keys. If Leo wanted to turn the whole place over it would have taken a long time. And he would have to have broken in. That's why I left the cabin unlocked the last few nights, as a bait.'

I grinned.

'I thought I told you to keep indoors at night. But I'll buy it. Human nature's a funny business.'

'You can say that again,' Alex Prosser said.

His eyes were fixed through the faint droplets of spray on the deckhouse glass as the hard-edged line of Bridport Inlet with its piers and lighthouse started coming up the far horizon.

'Do you think we'll ever sort this mess out, Mr Faraday?' he said.

'Maybe,' I said absently. 'As much as it ever will be. But I think we can satisfy the boys in blue. That's the important thing.'

I went on smoking and watching the skyline. It seemed like a hell of a long way back in.

3

'Only one corpse on the case, Mike,' Stella said.

I stared at her through my cigarette smoke as she sat the other side the desk, casually stirring her coffee.

'Oh, sure,' I said. 'What do you call Reardon and Leo Harris and Nikko and Grimaldi's boys and . . .'

'Don't go on,' Stella said with that maddeningly omniscient smile of hers. 'I was talking about your contribution to the proceedings. The man on Kathy Reardon's roof terrace.'

'Oh, that,' I said. 'Albert. I'd almost forgotten him.'

Stella looked at me in well-bred disgust. I grinned, ignoring her simulated indignation.

'Everyone gets an off-day once in a while. You could call it one of my quieter cases.'

Stella went on stirring her coffee in the dangerous silence which had fallen. It was warm and sunny today with a hard, metallic blue sky that even the smog couldn't subdue. The plastic-bladed fan went on turning with a sharp sound like it was trying to cut through pretzels. You're coming up with some pretty funny similes today, Mike, I told myself.

It had been a tough fortnight, what with the police inquiries and everything else. McGiver had been sore because I hadn't levelled with him but then he couldn't make it stick because I didn't know what the hell was going on myself most of the time. Diane Morris had talked and gone on talking. And the police had pieced together the rest through Holt.

Incredibly he had lived and was going to live. I'd been up to see him in the hospital and he'd been touchingly grateful. Like I told him he'd still be a comparatively young man when he came out. Especially by co-operating fully with the authorities. Like he'd said he'd managed to drive himself as far as Bridport Inlet the night he was shot. He'd collapsed near the pier where he was found by Leo Prosser and the girl who were staking-out the boat.

The story was roughly what Prosser and I

had already figured. So far as anyone was ever likely to know. Carter, the defecting courier, had stashed the diamonds. Holt's boys had decided to safeguard their own position by taking him out. Like I'd already learned Albert had jumped the gun.

So they had no diamonds and no location. That was when Grimaldi's New York mob sent Nikko down to whip the proceedings into shape. Albert had done his job in spades by killing Reardon too before getting the required information out of him. Nikko tried to go it alone, aware that his neck was also on the line.

I didn't know how he'd gotten on to Reardon's rented bungalow and neither did Kathy. Maybe through real estate firms. It was immaterial now anyway. But Nikko did no better than the Cocos people, especially when working under Holt's orders.

'What about Diane Morris?' Stella said.

My thoughts evaporated up on the ceiling with the smoke from my cigarette. I stared over toward the stalled automobiles on the boulevard below.

'What about her?'

Stella went on stirring her coffee mechanically.

'You know what I mean, Mike.'

I put down the stub of my cigarette in the earthenware tray on my desk and took the first sip of the coffee. Like always, it was great. I

212

stared at Stella through the dispersing haze. Today she wore a white silk blouse and a tailored grey skirt that set off her figure to perfection. The gold bell of her hair shimmered under the lamp as she shifted in her chair.

'I'm still waiting, Mike.'

'Diane Morris? She was the original poison belt. She made Lizabeth Scott, Ida Lupino and all those other hard ladies of nineteen forties Warner Brothers movies look like Mary Pickford. Money was the only thing that interested her. She'd been shacked up with Holt for some while and when he was searching for a safer place farther down the coast from Cocos she came to Bridport Inlet with him.

'That was when Leo Prosser was persuaded to throw in his lot with the local syndicate members. To Diane Morris he seemed a better proposition than Holt who, despite his flashy position as Cocos estate manager, had no real money of his own. Prosser had style; he was a smart accountant; and a partner with his brothers in one of the most prosperous boat-building and hire companies on the coast.'

'So she took over Prosser,' Stella said.

I nodded.

'Installing herself a short distance away as a cafe waitress. The perfect cover. And she was always available for Prosser. The couple used to meet well away from Bridport Inlet so no-one there was in the know, though Alex Prosser had his suspicions. The couple had an apartment in a western section of downtown L.A. Things went well at first. Prosser was augmenting his income with runs for the syndicate. But Miss Morris' extravagance soon had him siphoning off the funds of Prosser Marine.'

Stella shrugged, sipping delicately at her brew.

'But the firm will survive?'

'I guess so,' I said. 'Prosser has the best help available and it's certain he'll never come to trial for his brother's death. My evidence and that of Holt alone would make sure of that.'

Stella nodded, her very blue eyes staring me out.

'Why would Reardon want to go to Prosser's boatyard, a place so far away?'

'Because he knew the people around Cocos were in the syndicate's pay,' I said. 'Just an odd coincidence, which sometimes happens.'

'So where are the diamonds, Mike?'

I grinned.

'That map reference put them just on the northern tip of Cocos. They were under the noses of Albert and Holt and Nikko all the time. McGiver only released the information to me this morning. They had to be tactful about Harrison.'

'Where does he stand?' Stella said.

'Nowhere,' I told her. 'He's currently in

214

Europe and my guess is he'll stay there until this whole thing blows over. But I don't think he's personally involved and neither does McGiver.'

'So they got the diamonds up?' Stella said.

'Sure, with the help of Dad Corcoran, one of the local boat-hire wizards.'

I smiled again.

'It was right on the edge of a difficult landing place where I went ashore on that trip with Corcoran. The guy had simply added another navigation buoy to the set guarding the channel through the rocks. The stuff was only a few fathoms down at low tide. And no-one would ever have bothered to count the number of buoys there.'

'Smart stuff,' Stella said. 'You thought Lionel Prosser might have been involved.'

I eased more coffee down me, conscious that I could still feel a slight twinge in my leg. All my other bruises had long disappeared.

'That's true,' I told her. 'After we had that little disagreement in the cabin I figured he might have been trying to stop me searching those chart books. But that was long after we'd come to blows. It shows how wrong one can be.'

'Just my sentiments,' Stella said cheerfully.

She got up and bent over to pick up my cup from the blotter. Her lips brushed my forehead and then she'd skipped out before I could grab her. She was upsetting my concentration this afternoon.

'What time are we due at the Prossers' tonight?'

'Around seven,' I said. 'We'll leave here at five and go straight to your place. That will give you half an hour to shower and change. Providing Kathy Reardon's on time.'

Stella smiled again. I could have watched it all day.

'Why the early start?'

'We're to meet the whole family,' I said. 'And there's something special in the way of a drinking session before we tackle the food.'

Stella gave me a little moue.

'Sounds dangerously like an orgy, Mike.'

She went over to the alcove to fetch my second cup.

'Not a bad idea,' I said. 'We've never been to an orgy together.'

'There's always the first time,' she said in a dangerous voice.

I sat back at the desk, thinking over the heavy case; of a hitherto honest accountant destroyed by a woman who made him first an embezzler, then a murderer. It was a deadly world all right.

'What do you think I ought to wear?' Stella said.

I tried to stare her out, failed.

'Mink at least,' I said. 'I forgot to tell you Prosser's presenting me with a bonus cheque tonight. To express his gratitude, he said. He's turned the Prosser enterprise into a public company and a Government agency and a private consortium have come up with the money to put the business back on its feet.'

'Faraday Enterprises could do with a little of that themselves,' Stella said.

'That'll be the day,' I told her.

I looked down at the stalled traffic again.

'Still, things aren't so bad. If the cheque's big enough I'll maybe come out with enough to buy myself a new truss.'

Stella's smile lasted all the way to the ground floor as we rode down in the elevator.

We hope you have enjoyed this Large Print book. Other Chivers Press or G.K. Hall & Co. Large Print books are available at your library or directly from the publishers.

For more information about current and forthcoming titles, please call or write, without obligation, to:

Chivers Press Limited
Windsor Bridge Road
Bath BA2 3AX
England
Tel. (01225) 335336

OR

G.K. Hall & Co.
P.O. Box 159
Thorndike, Maine 04986
USA
Tel. (800) 223-2336

All our Large Print titles are designed for easy reading, and all our books are made to last.